The Secret of Jerry's Pride

The Secret of Jerry's Pride

JO A. TOTTY

ReadersMagnet, LLC

The Secret of Jerry's Pride
Copyright © 2021 by Jo A. Totty

Published in the United States of America
ISBN Paperback: 978-1-954371-65-1
ISBN ebook: 978-1-954371-64-4

All rights reserved. No part of this publication may be reproduced, stored in a retrieval system or transmitted in any way by any means, electronic, mechanical, photocopy, recording or otherwise without the prior permission of the author except as provided by USA copyright law.

This is a work of fiction. Names, characters, places and incidents either are the product of the author's imagination or are used fictitiously, and any resemblance to any actual persons, living or dead, events or locales is entirely coincidental.

ReadersMagnet, LLC
10620 Treena Street, Suite 230 | San Diego, California, 92131 USA
1.619.354.2643 | www.readersmagnet.com

Book design copyright © 2021 by ReadersMagnet, LLC. All rights reserved.
Cover design by Kent Gabutin
Interior design by Renalie Malinao

Dedication

Dedicated to my sister Betty Dreaden, who died March 1, 2011. She was my best friend and supporter.

Chapter 1

The door opened very slowly as Lucy Benson slipped quietly into the border's room. She knew she wasn't suppose to be there. She had been told many times but she had to find out Mr. Peters's secret. She knew he was hiding something in his room and she was determined to find out what it was.

All of this had started six months ago when Mr. Peters had come to town.

It was a small town in Middle Tennessee called Newleyville. It was June, nineteen and forty three.

Mrs. Nora Benson ran the only boarding house in Newleyville. She was a widow with four children to raise alone. Her husband had been killed three years ago in a logging accident. This was her way to support her children. The house was very large, and she now had six borders.

Newleyville boasted a grocery store, a barber shop, a doctor's office, a department store, that doubled as a general store where you could find anything needed on the farm or in a home.

It had all started several months ago, when John Peters had first come to town. He was a tall man about six foot four inches tall and weighed around two hundred pounds. He had dark black hair and black piercing eyes, that seemed to look through you. He very seldom smiled and when he did the smile never reached his eyes. He spoke in a deep, low voice and talked very little to anyone.

Nobody in town knew him or anything about him. He had no relatives that lived there and no one knew why he was in town. He just showed up one day, got a room at the boarding house and was still there. He didn't work anywhere but he had always paid his rent on time and seemed to have money for what he needed

He had received two letters since he had arrived, but neither had a return address.

Every afternoon around five o'clock he went for a walk. He would be gone for about an hour and a half, then he returned and went to his room. He didn't leave his room until around seven the next morning when he came down for breakfast.

One afternoon he entered the grocery store. As usual a group of men from town were there sitting and talking. In any small southern town, the grocery store was the gathering place for the men of the community. Tom Billings was the owner of the store. He was a small man and everybody called him "Pee Wee."

Pee Wee said, "Almost everybody knows where the Newleys live. It's about three miles from town on Newley Road. It's a big white house with big columns on the front porch. It set back off of the road a piece, but you can't miss it. There's no bigger house around here than the Newley's house."

"Thank you, sir", Mr. Peters said as he walked out of the store, letting the screen door slam behind him.

"Wonder what he wanted to know that fer." Slim said.

"What I wonder is how he knows Smith Newley," said Pee Wee. "They are people with money and that feller don't appear to be somebody like that."

For quite a while that was the topic of the conversation at the store until "Pee Wee" got busy waiting on some customers, who had come in to buy their weeks groceries.

Meanwhile Mr. Peters was on his way to the Newley home. He didn't think that they would remember him because he was just a boy the last time they had seen him. He remembered Smith Newley alright. He would never forget how he looked. The color of his eyes, his every feature, how he walked and the sound of his voice. No, he would never forget Smith Newley.

The closer he got to the Newley's place the more disturbed he became. He went over everything in his mind over and over. Finally, he turned around and started back to the Boarding House. He never made it to the Newley's place. At least not that day.

Meanwhile, Lucy had just gone into Peters room, suddenly the door to his room opened and her mother walked in. "Lucy! What are you doing in this room? You know you are never to go into a boarder's room. Young lady, you get out of here this very minute. If I catch you even close to a boarder's room again you are going to be in big trouble. Now, you get downstairs and get busy peeling potatoes for supper. Now get!"

Lucy started to say something but she went on downstairs, and did as she had been told, but she thought "I'll get my chance to find out what he is hiding in that room. I swear I will!" Mrs. Benson came out of the room and closed the door behind her. "What am I going to do with that girl?" She went on down stairs and into the kitchen. It was time to start cooking supper for the boarders.

Miss Sally Bookers was one of the boarders. She was a twenty one year old, young lady, who was the school teacher for the children of the town. she was a very pretty, young lady with long blond hair and big blue eyes. When she smiled the deep dimples in each cheek made her face light up. She was small in stature but had a heart as big as a mountain. She was a friend to everyone in town and well known for her good deeds.

Mr. Peters came down for supper that night, for the first time since he had been there. He happened to be seated next to Miss Booker. She introduced herself to him and tried to carry on a conversation but all she got from him was a grunt or two. Finally she gave up and ate the rest of her supper in silence. She had never met anyone like him before.

Peters kept pretty much to his same routine for the next several weeks. Still taking his afternoon walks and still being a loner, not making friends with anyone. When people tried to become friendly with him, he would either ignore them or walk away.

One afternoon John Peters entered the grocery store. He got a drink out of the ice box and caried it to the counter to pay for it. There he told "Pee WEE" he wanted some peanuts to go with the coke and he paid him for the coke and the bag of peanuts.

"Say, did you have any problem finding the Newley's house that you were asking about not long ago?" Pee Wee asked.

"I didn't go that far," Peters answered. After saying that he took his coke and bag of peanuts and left the store.

"Now, what do you fellows make of that?" Pee Wee asked the men in the store.

"I do believe that's the strangest man I've ever seen in my life," Slim said.

I believe he's more than a little strange. I think he's about half crazy!" Zeke said.

"Let me tell you fellows this much. I believe he's a dangerous man." Pee Wee said. "We'd better keep an eye on him. No telling what he's libel to do. He could go off one day, and hurt somebody bad. You never know what somebody like that has on their mind."

Slim said, "you're right Pee Wee. I heard tell about a feller who lived back in the woods. He was a lot like Peters. It was a long time ago but my daddy told me about it. That feller killed a whole family of people. Shot em one by one. When the law found him, he was crazy as a bat. They never did find out why he had done it. They couldn't make head or tails out of what he told them. He died in the asylum a few years after that. That family didn't even know that man."

It got quiet in the store, each man lost in his own thoughts.

Chapter 2

Summer turned into fall earlier that year than usual. It had been very dry during July and August and when September came the pastures were almost gone. The hay crops were almost non-existent. All of the farmers were worried how they would make it through the long winter ahead.

October came and with it came rain. The days were warmer than usual and the pastures began to grow again. The trees began to change color of their leaves, but they were not as bright that year, because it had been so dry, for so long.

After about a week of heavy rain, the skies cleared and the sun came out. The days were sunny and warm but after the sun went down the nights were growing cooler.

Farmers began to cut what hay they had, and get it into the barns. Because of the dry weather during the growing season, the corn crops hadn't done very well. After the frosts came the farmers began to gather what little corn crops, they had left, in the fields. None of them had very much corn left to salvage.

During all this time, John Peters had remained in Newleyvile. He still followed his same routine and still remained a loner. He took his walks every day regardless of the weather. The men at the store noticed that he was going in a different direction than he had been going before.

One day when he had stopped in at the store to pick up a few things Slim said, "Mr. Peters, I've noticed that you've changed to a different direction for your walks now. Decide to see some more of our town?"

Mr. Peters turned around and looked straight at Slim and said, "got tired of seeing the same thing every day, so I changed it. Is there anything wrong with that?"

"No sir, not a thing" Slim said. "The way you're walking now has a lot of pretty places to see. I think you will like it."

Without another word Mr. Peters left the store.

"Well, Slim, I don't think Mr. Peters liked your question very much," Pee Wee said.

"Did you see the look in that man's eyes when he looked at me?" Slim asked. "He scared the fire out of me! I don't want that man mad at me."

"He would not be a man you would want as an enemy," Zeke said.

What the men at the store didn't know was that as soon as Mr. Peters was out of sight of the store, he headed straight into the woods. He walked about four miles back in the woods until he came to a little shack. On the outside it looked like no one had lived there for years.

The shack was set back against a hill. He opened the door and went inside. It, too, looked as if no one had lived there for years. He went to the back and moved some boards that were there. After he had done that, he was inside a room that had been dug out in the hillside. He very carefully replaced the boards to the back of the shack.

Inside, the dug out place in the hillside, was a door that opened into a very large room that had also been dug out. Walls had been put up and a wooden floor had been put down. The back of the room had been left open and as he moved out of the back room he entered a large cave. The farther back in the cave he went, the bigger it became.

There was a spring that emptied into a crystal clear pool. He lit torches that were fitted into each side of the walls of the cave.

Furniture was in the front part of the entrance , and in this area a small pit had been dug out, in the limestone floor of the cave, for cooking.

"Are you here?" Peters called out.

"Yes, John, I'm here," a woman's voice answered. From out of the shadows walked an old woman. Her shoulders were stooped and she limped as she walked with a cane. Following close behind her was an old man, who appeared to be blind.

Peters walked up to her and put his arms around her. Then turning to the old man he did the same.

"Are you both all right?" he asked.

The woman answered, "Yes, John, we're doing fine. Paw ate a good breakfast this morning and he is much stronger today."

"Come on, let's go sit down and talk for a while. I'll fix us some supper in a little while."

They all went to the front room and sat down in the chairs that were there.

"It's always warm and cozy in here," the old man said. "We never know what the weather is like outside."

"Today it's kind of cold out there. There's a nip in the air and the wind is out of the north," John said. ""Winter is beginning to move in, I'm afraid."

"It won't bother us, any. We've got a warm, dry place to stay and you've brought us plenty of food to have to eat. Did any of the people you've stole all of this canned stuff, and the eggs, and meat from the smoke house, ever find out where it went?" the old woman asked.

"Maw, they have no idea that I took it. Nobody ever saw me around the places and nobody ain't seen me with anything. So how could they know?" John asked. "Is there anything that you need?"

"Naw, we're fine and set for the winter. You might bring in some more wood before you go. We're a little low on wood for me to use for cooking." the old woman said.

"Was that enough coal-oil to last through winter to light the lamps? Peters asked.

"Yeah, we go to bed early ever night, so we don't use very much," she answered.

"Let me heat up supper so you can eat and I can get back before it gets dark I'll eat supper at the Boarding House, tonight," Peters said. "I'll go get you some wood, then I'll head on back."

He went outside and in a little while he came back with as much wood as he could carry in his arms. After making three or four trips outside and bringing back wood each time, he soon had a large pile of sticks and branches. He had it all broken so it would fit in the fire pit.

"I'd best be going. I'll be back tomorrow and I'll bring you some cofffee," Peters said.

After giving both of the old couple a hug, he said, "Now don't go outside. You don't know who might be out in these woods hunting. You might get shot. You're safe here and nobody in a hundred years would find you. I'll see you tomorrow."

With those words he walked out of the room, through the shack and dissapeared into the woods.

John made his way out of the woods and back into town in time to eat supper at the Boarding House.

Chapter 3

Mr. Newley had come into the grocery store with a grocery list his wife had given him that morning.

"Good morning, fellows," he said. "How are things going in town today? Pee Wee, are you keeping all of these fellows out of trouble?"

"Now, Mr. Newley, you know that nobody can keep these boys out of trouble. Some of them are so ornery can't nobody do nothing with them," Pee Wee said. "Now, you take Zeke , there, he's so ornery his own dog bites him every time he goes home."

All of the men laughed at that. Zeke was a shy, humble man that everybody liked. He just grined when they teased him.

Slim spoke up, "Say, Mr. Newley, that John Peters was asking where you lived, a while back. Did he ever come to your place?"

"No, Slim, I don't know any John Peters, but nobody has been to the place that I didn't know." Mr. Newley said. "I got some of the neighbors to help us get the crops gathered and put in the barns, but I've known them for years. What did this John Peters want any way?""He didn't say," Pee Wee said. "But he don't say much to anybody, any how. He's a strange man. He's been here for over six months and don't nobody know nothing about him. He don't work or nothing."

"Now, that is strange," Mr. Newley said. "I'll keep my eyes pleeled for a stranger. Are you through filling my list, Pee Wee? The wife will think I got lost. She said she needed some things for dinner. I don't want no trouble with the little woman."

Mr. Newley paid "Pee Wee" for his groceries and left the store on his way home.

After he was gone the men talked about what a nice person Mr. Newley was, and how well liked he was by the people in the community.

It was about a week later that John Peters came in the grocery store and told "Pee Wee" he needed a list of supplies for about a week. He handed him a list of the things he would need.

"I'm going camping for about a week." Peters said.

"It's getting a little cold for camping," Pee Wee said.

Peters said, "This is the kind of weather I like to camp out. I've got good equipment and I'll be fine. I do this every year around this time of year."

"Pee Wee" filled the order he had been given and told Mr. Peters how much the bill was. Mr. Peters paid the bill and left the store.

"Pee Wee" said, "Mr. Peters was long winded today. I don't think I've heard him talk that much in all of the months he's been here. I wonder where he's going camping."

"Ain't no place around here that ain't private property. Ain't nobody going to want him camping on their land this time of year," Slim said.

"Knowing how he is, he ain't going to care how they feel about it. He'll do it any way. Trespassing ain't going to bother him none," Zeke said.

"If he's on my land I sure ain't going to try to run him off," "Pee Wee" said.

That started all of the men laughing, and they started teasing "Pee Wee" about him running through the bushes with bullets whizzing around his head.

Before much time had passed, they watched as Peters came by with a huge pack on his back. He went in the same direction he had been taking for a while now.

Just as he had done often before, as soon as he was out of sight of the store, Peters went into the woods.

After walking about four miles back into the woods, he came to the old shack. He went in and out through the back and into the dug out. He went on into the cave and put his back pack down. He sat there for a few minutes to rest before removing the things from the pack.

The old man and the old lady came from the shadows of the cave.

"John, we wanted to be sure that it was you before we came out," the old woman said.

"I've brought a bunch of groceries this time. I got some candy and stuff like that. I also got coffee, meal, flour, sugar and Paw, I brought you a jar of honey. There's some butter in there too. Maw, I'll get it all out and put it up for you in a little while. It was a heavy load to carry this far," John said.

"Lord, have mercy, won't we have a feast tonight, Paw.?" the old woman asked.

"I'm going to stay for a while this time. I'll stay for a week. There's a lot I need to do here to get you ready for the winter. Oh, yeah, I brought a box of matches this time," John said. "I noticed you didn't have many left in the box the last time I was here."

"That's right! I forgot to tell you we were almost out of matches," the old man said."I've kept some flint we could use if we run out of matches."

John went about putting away the groceries that he had brought in the backpack. Before very long, he had everything put in its place. There was plenty of everything they would need to make it through the winter, even if it turned out to be a long one.

After he had taken care of the groceries, he went outside to gather wood for the cooking pit. It would take a large amount in case they needed to use it as heat.

He came in with arm load after arm load until he had two large stacks against the wall of one side of the cave. A lot of it, he had cut up with a small hatchet. All of it was dry, dead, wood so it would burn hot without very much smoke.

Of all of his trips there, he had never seen any trace of any other humans who had been near the old shack. He was always sure not to take the same path each trip so it would not leave any trace of anyone passing through there.

It would never do for the old couple to be discovered. That would destroy all of the well laid plans.

Some time during the night it started to rain. The rain fell hard all the rest of the night and it was still raining when John looked out the next morning.

"There will be no going outside today. We can't take a chance on leaving any tracks," John said.

"We don't never go outside this way. A long way back at the other end there is a opening that comes out on the side of a hill. You can't see it from the outside . It's all covered with bushes and stuff. When we go outside that's the way we go," the old man said.

John said, "I'll check that out before I leave. I didn't know that was back there. As long as it can't be seen from the outside, it's O.K.."

The week seemed to move quickly. It rained for two days in a row. Most of the leaves had fallen from the trees and it was getting colder each day.

At night after supper they would sit by the cooking fire and talk until it was time to go to bed. They relived their past lives and planned their future.

A lot of events had happened in their lives that could have been prevented. They had lost their home because they would not hold a job for more than a month at a time. Then they would get fired, for one reason or another, and not get another one for two or three months. They could not pay their bills and therefore the bank had foreclosed on their house. They blamed all of their misfortune on everyone but themselves.

They had started stealing from stores and homes and had left the place where they had lived just as the police were closing in on them.

They had traveled from town to town picking up odd jobs and staying for a while until they were in danger of getting caught, then moving on.

John had finally got into bigger things. He was robbing stores, banks, service stations and stealing money from people using a gun.

He was robbing a house one night when he thought no one was home but they were there. As he came in the window the man was standing there with a shotgun aimed at John. As he dived through the window to escape, the man pulled the trigger on the shotgun and had hit him in the leg. He wasn't hit directly so he ran away without getting caught.

Of course the family had to move on quickly. It took a long time for John's leg to heal because he wouldn't go to a doctor for fear that the doctor would turn him in to the police.

Finally, they were settled in a small town in Kentucky. John left after his leg healed enough for him to travel.

He had wandered around Kentucky working on horse ranches, cleaning the stalls, feeding the horses and being a handy man for years.

He had met a pretty, young girl on one of the ranches. She was the rancher's daughter and her name was Lettie Woodrow. She was about five feet seven inches tall with jet black hair that fell in curls down her back. She had the bluest eyes fringed with black eyelashes. She was one of the prettist girls in Kentucky and her Daddy's pride and joy.

Half of the young men who worked on the ranch were in love with her but for some reason Lettie didn't think of them as anything but men who worked on the ranch.

When John started working there, he would tip his hat to her and just keep walking. He wasn't like the other men. At that time in his life he was a very handsome man. He was always quiet and didn't have much to say to anyone, especially Lettie. The more he ignored her, the more she liked him.

When the other men had a day off they would head to town but John never went with them. He stayed in the bunk house or went riding on one of the horses. He was content just to be by himself. He did whatever the Boss asked him to do and did a good job without complaining. The horses seemed to like him and he could get them to do whatever he asked of them, without ever raising his voice.

Chapter 4

One day when John was out riding, Lettie had followed him on her horse. She had stayed back a distance until they were a mile or two from the ranch house. Then she came riding up at hard gallop. "Hello, John. I didn't know you were riding out this way. I thought I would give Ruley a good work out today. She hasn't had a good run for quiet a while," she said.

"It's a good day for that today. The weather is just the temperature to keep from getting too hot when she' going at a hard run. Lots of people don't think about that until it's too late," John said.

"Horses are a lot like people, if they are driven too hard, for too long, they will break," he said. Then he started to ride off.

Lettie rode her horse up to where he was. "How did you get so smart about horses? Who are you, John Peters? Who are you, really?" she asked.

"No, there is a lot more to you than the eye can see, John Peters," she said. "I know that and you're different from the other men who work here. You are a mystery I haven't yet solved, but I will."

"You know as much about me as you need to know. Let it go "Miss Lettie". Just let it be. There can never be anything between us but what there is now. I"m a loner and I"ll always be a loner. Don't try to make me anything else. It won't work. Like I said, just let it be." After saying this John took off at a hard gallop back toward the ranch house.

"You are a strange man, John Peters," Lettie said, "A very strange man, indeed".

She continued on her way. She thought about the conversation between her and John Peters. Maybe he was right about her letting things be as they were now. He appeared to be a dangerous man if he got upset about anything. He wasn't worth her taking any chances. Her Daddy always said, 'Let sleeping dogs lie." This time she had better take her Daddy's advice.

John had made his way back to the barn. He had also been thinking about the conversation between him and Lettie. He felt like she was trouble with a capital T. He didn't need any woman getting too close to him. They got too nosey and that was the last thing he needed. He didn't need anybody digging into his past. He had much, too much to hide. If she started asking questions she might ask the wrong person and that would be trouble for him.

The best thing for him to do was leave this place. He'd get his things together before the men got back from town. He could hide his stuff in the barn until he got ready to go later tonight. He'd wait until the men went to bed, then he'd slip out and be gone before anybody knew about him leaving. By morning he'd have a lot of miles between him and the ranch. Nobody would know the direction he went in, so it would be wise to take the direction they wouldn't think he'd go.

He knew exactly where he would go. In his rides over the ranch he had located a hidden cave just outside the ranch property. He'd hide out there for a couple of weeks and then move on. They wouldn't waste much time looking for him, if they looked for him at all.

Lettie returned her horse to the barn. She took her saddle off the horse and rubbed the horse down good. Then she put her horse in the stall and fed and watered her. Then she headed for the ranch house to get ready for supper. John had watched Lettie while she took care of her horse from his hiding place in the barn loft. He had already fed and watered the rest of the horses. His stuff was safely hidden in the barn loft. Now all he had left to do was eat his supper and wait until it was time to leave.

The men began to drift back to the ranch two or three at a time. By the time supper was ready, to go on the table, they were all home.

It was quiet at the supper table that night. The men were all tired from their trip to town and all they wanted to do was eat and get to bed to catch up on their lost sleep. As they had come in, John had told them that he had taken care of all the feeding and watering of the horses. They would have no work to do tonight.

Soon supper was over and the men began to get up and leave the kitchen to go to the bunkhouse to get ready for bed. The Boss had said that tomorrow would be a full day of work. They had a lot of fencing that had to be done.

The Secret of Jerry's Pride

A lot of the fences were getting old and would have to be replaced. Before they started that, all of the horses would have to be moved to another pasture.

All during supper Lettie had hot spoken a word to John. She had glanced his way several times but her conversation was directed to her father or one of the men at the table.

As soon as John finished eating, he got up from the table and went out the kitchen door without saying a word to anyone. Nobody thought anything about it because that was what he usually did when supper was over.

He went straight to the bunkhouse and lay down on his bed. Most of the rest of the men had already gone to bed. It was already dark outside and some of them were asleep. The ones who were still awake were either reading or talking quietly to the person in the bed next to them. John picked up a magazine that was laying on the table next to his bed and started reading it.

It wasn't long until all of the men were in bed and all of the lights had been turned off. Soon John heard all of them snoring. He stayed in his bed for about thirty more minutes to make sure that they were sleeping soundly. Then he got out of bed, walked to the door, very quietly opened it and slipped out into the darkness.

He went by the barn, picked up his clothes, in the backpack, from the barn loft where he hidden it earlier. Now he was ready to be on his way.

He looked outside to make sure that no one was wandering around. Then he looked at the ranch house to see if any lights were still on. There were no lights on.

He walked out into the darkness and started the long walk to the cave. If he kept up at a good fast pace he should be at the cave about two to three hours before daylight. He had been to the cave many times before when he was out riding but he never went up to the cave. He had kept it in mind in case he ever needed to get away.

It was about three hours before daylight when John reached the mouth of the cave. Bushes had grown up until you couldn't see the cave. If he hadn't known what to look for he would never have seen the enterance the first time when he had found it.

John had always been fascinated with caves. When he was a very young boy he had been able to locate a cave just by looking at the lay of the land. He never missed when he told the other boys where a cave was just by looking at the area around the cave.

He climbed up the hill where he knew the cave would be. Sure enough after carefully going around the bushes there was the opening to the cave. He went inside and lit the lantern he had brought with him. The cave was one big room. Near the back was a spring that came out of the side of the cave and then went into an underground stream.

He took some food from the backpack that he had put in the afternoon before and ate a portion of it. Then he rolled out his bed roll and lay down to get some sleep. He was tired after his walk to the cave. He would sleep for a while then get up and check the cave out more. He put the lantern out, closed his eyes and in a few minutes he was sound asleep.

It was early afternoon when John woke up. He felt refreshed after his nap. He got up and streched to get the kincks out of his body. He'd forgotten what it was like not sleeping on a bed. He went to the opening of the cave and looked out.

Directly in front of the cave was a herd of horses being herded by six men on horseback. He quickly moved farther back in the cave but could still see the horses and the men. None of the men had ever glanced at the hillside. They were busy watching the horses. John thought they were moving the horses to a new pasture or getting ready to sell them. He remembered that a big horse sale was coming up next week.

The men kept the horses moving across the pasture until they were out of sight. He knew they wouldn't be coming back this way for at least two weeks. Then they'd bring in a new herd of mares. So he knew he had plenty of time to rest up before he moved on.

The time John stayed at the cave passed quickly for him. He was well rested and ready to move on.

Chapter 5

John had made his way out of Kentucky and into Tennessee by hitching rides.

One couple who had picked him up were on their way to Nashville to visit the woman's mother. So John told them that he also had relatives in Nashvile and that is where he was going. He said he was on leave from the Army and that it would be a month before he had to report in at Fort Bragg. He was going to spend some time with his family before going on to his next assignment .

When they reached Nashville he told them to let him out at the Greyhound Bus Station because his sister was to pick him up there. They dropped him off at the station and went on their way.

He stayed in Nashville for almost a week but it was crowded and had too many policemen everywhere. He was afraid he would be recognized by one of the policemen and so he decided to move on.

After traveling around for a few months he was in Newleyville. It was the ideal place for John. The law would never find him here.

He took a room at the Boarding House and had been there since then. Nobody bothered him and he could take his time and get everything perfect this time. He had been thinking about this job since he had found out about the people being in this area. Revenge would be sweet.

After he had been in town for about two weeks he contacted his parents. He wanted to find a place for them so that no one would know they were here. During his walks he had serached until he had found the old shack and the cave behind it. When he had it ready, he sent word to his parents.

They came into town around eleven o'clock one night. He met them and carried them to the cave. They had remained there since then.

He would need them when the time came to carry out his plan. He had everything planned, all he had to do now, was wait for the right time to carry it all out. It was perfect and there was no way he would ever be caught. It was fool proof and afterwards he and his parents could go away somwhere and live a life of ease. They would be somebody who was respected.

After staying for a week with his parents he packed his things and went back to the Boarding House. It was late afternoon when he got back in town.

The next morning he went by the grocery store.

"Good Morning, Mr. Peters. How was your camping trip?" Pee Wee asked.

"Fine," Mr. Peters replied.

"We had some rain while you were gone," Slim said.

"Yeah, it did rain two days," Mr. Peters said.

He got his uaual drink and bag of peanuts, paid for them and left the store.

"He was real talkative this morning, wasn't he?" Slim said.

"Yeah, his trip really did wonders for him. Did you notice what a good mood he was in?" Pee Wee said laughing.

"If that man had a good mood in his life I sure would like to be there to see it," Zeke said. "He wouldn't know what it was and it would probably make him sick."

"Oh, well some people are just born in a bad mood and never out grow it," Pee Wee said.

"Yeah, like ole Zeke there. Bless his heart," Slim said. Everybody laughed at that. Zeke was known for his good nature.

Chapter 6

"Pee Wee"and his wife Ester had two sons. Both of them were grown up and no longer lived at home.

Tom, their oldest son was a Deputy for the sheriff of their county. He was twenty four years old and had gone into Law Enforcement right after graduation from high school.

Jim, their youngest son had gone on to college and became an agent for the Tennessee Bureau of Investigation. He was now twenty two and had been working for about a year.

Every year when vacation time came, they would come home to visit their parents for a week or sometimes two. Neiher of them had married and they woud try to get their vacations at the same time.

Zeke came into the store one morning in early spring to have his usual cup of coffee with Pee Wee and the other men gathered there. They were sitting and talking and the subject turned to their families.

"Say "Pee Wee", how are your boys doing? I haven't heard you say much about them lately," Zeke asked.

"They're both fine," Pee Wee said. "They're coming home next month. They're taking their vacations and are going to come home to see me and Ester."

"Are they still in the law business?" Slim asked.

"Yeah," "PeeWee" said. "Both of them have good jobs and make a good living. Neither of them has got married yet. They both work a lot of hours. One of them is sometimes on a job for a month or more without coming home. You know that don't set well with a wife."

Zeke said, "Don't tell Bertha about that work. She'll be trying to get me a job with them people."

The men really laughed at what Zeke had said. He laughed as hard as they did.

"Bertha wouldn't trade you for a farm in Texas," Slim said.

All of the men knew Bertha and her gentle way. They knew she loved Zeke for his gentle way and his sense of humor. Everybody in the community thought a lot of the couple because they were both as kind-hearted as could be. They were a childless couple but all of the children in the community loved them and called them "Uncle Zeke" and "Aunt Bertha".

While they were talking Smith Newley entered the store.

"Howdy, Mr. Newley, come on in. Zeke is rare form today. He thinks Bertha wants to get rid of him. We all know Bertha couldn't run him off," "Pee Wee" said. "She couldn't get shed of him if she wanted to."

"It sounds to me as if Zeke isn't the only one who is in rare form," Mr. Newley said. "You boys all seem to be having a good time today. It's nice to see."

"What can I get for you today?" "Pee Wee" asked.

"Mrs. Newley has quiet a long list today, "Pee Wee". If you would get this list together for me, I would appreciate it," Mr. Newley said, handing "Pee Wee" a paper with a long list of items written on it.

"Yes, sir," "Pee Wee" said. "I'll fix you, right up."

As "Pee Wee" gathered the items, Mr. Newley talked to the men. He told them about the ten head of cattle he had just purchased and the four new horses he had bought from a horse farm in Kentucky.

By this time "Pee Wee" had Mr. Newley's order filled and the bill waiting for him. Mr. Newley paid the bill, gathered up the bags of groceries and with "Pee Wee" helping him carry out some of the bags, put them in his truck and went on his way home.

"PeeWee" went back ito the store. "I sure could use a lot more customers like Mr. Newley. He spends a lot of his money here and he's such a nice man. Have any of you fellows ever met Mrs. newley? She is really a pretty lady, young too. A lot younger than he is I would say."

"Naw, I ain't never seen her," Zeke said.

"Me, neither," Slim said. "How long have they been here?"

"It's about ten years now I think," Zeke said. "I remember when they moved here. Mr. Newley came here and stayed at the Boarding House while the house was being built. It was built quick, a lot of men worked on it and didn't stop until everything was done."

"I remember that, now," Slim said. "They even had a man who put the rocks down to walk on and he put all of them roses out. He set out a lot of flowers and made little paths so you could walk through and look at the flowers. He put them white statues in the back yard. I never did understand why they wanted them things setting out there. Funny people wanting all them figures setting out there!"

"Well, I got to get on home before Bertha feeds my supper to Shep," Zeke said.

"Me, too," Slim said, "but not cause Bertha wll feed my supper to Shep."

Both of the men left the store laughing. "See you tomorrow "PeeWee"," they both said at the same time.

"Pee Wee" stayed at the store for about half an hour after the men left. He only had two more customers after that. Two young boys came in and bought a piece of candy, each. After they left, "Pee Wee" closed the store and went home to eat his supper.

Chapter 7

John had been keeping a low profile for a while. He went for his walks every day but he was staying close to the Boarding House. He was getting closer to carrying out his well laid plans. The time seemed to be almost right.

Lucy hadn't forgotten about getting into Mr. Peter's room. She had been planning for several months on how to get into his room. He seemed to always be around lately. The next time he left the house she was going into that room!

It wasn't long after that, Mr. Peters left his room and went out the front door. Lucy watched as he passed the grocery store. She knew he was going on his usual walk. Now was her chance. She went running up the steps and headed to Mr. Peters' room. She reached the door, opened it and stepped inside closing the door behind her.

She looked around the room. It had clothes thrown on the chair. The bed was rumpled and the covers were thrown up on the bed. She looked at the dresser . The top was littered with pieces of rumpled note paper. She walked over, picked up one of the rumpled papers, smoothed it out and read it. It said, "slip into the house after dark, go to bedroom, put the knife to throat, hand over mouth, remember to get____". About that time Lucy heard a noise. She ran to the door and listened to see if steps were coming to that door. The steps were getting fainter and she knew someone was going down the steps.

She stuffed the papers in her pocket, opened the door and slipped out. Quickly she ran away from the door and down the stairs. Soon she was in the kitchen to help her mother get the supper ready for the boarders.

About five minutes later Peters came in the front door and went upstairs to his room. He opened the door and walked into the room. He felt as if something was different but he didn't know what. He looked all around the room but didn't see anything different than he had left it. Oh, well, he was just nervous. He had become leary of everyone and everything. He had to settle down or people would know something was wrong.

Later, he heard the call that supper was on the table. He went downstairs, went to the table and sat down to eat. Mrs. Benson had green beans, corn, creamed potatoes, a pork roast and corn-bread and chocolate cake for supper that night. Everyone ate with a hearty appetite. Most of the boarders told Mrs. Benson how much they enjoyed the supper. Peters, as usual, made no comment. He got up from the table and walked up to his room. A little while later, he went to bed.

Later that night after everybody was asleep, he got out of bed and slipped downstairs and out the front door. He went quickly in the same direction he took on his walks.

It was around eleven o'clock when he reached his destination. The house was dark and quiet. He slipped around the house to the back. He looked at all of the windows to see if any of them were open. They were not. He checked everything about the house, the barn and all of the sheds. He sat in the back yard for a while watching the house. Then he left and arrived back at the Bording House long before any of the people were awake.

Chapter 8

The Smithering family was a family that had moved ino a house about a mile down the road from where the Newley family lived. They had been living there for two years.

The Smithering family consisted of Jethro, his wife Lizzy, and their two children Jenny their daughter, who was twenty six years old and their son Jerry, who was twenty three. Neither of the children were married, at least not that anyone knew about. They were a quiet faimily, who kept pretty much to themselves. They were friendly, enough but really had no close friends.

Jethro and Jerry both worked for Mr. Newley. They helped him with the farm work and took care of the cattle and horses. Jerry seemed to have a special gift when it came to the horses. He could get them to do just what he wanted them to, by simply talking to them. Some of them would not let anybody but Jerry ride them.

Jenny worked for Mrs. Newley. She did the laundry, washing and ironing. She also cleaned house for her three days a week.

Jenny was a pretty girl, with long, curly, brown hair and soft brown eyes. She smiled easily and had such a pretty smile. She was sweet natured and got along well with everyone.

One day Mr. Smithering came to the grocery store to pick up some groceries for his family.

He said, "Hello, fellows. How are you all doing? "Pee Wee", I have a list of groceries we need. Would you get this list together for me?"

"Yes sir. I'll have them for you in a few minutes," "Pee Wee" said.

He began to gather up the items that Mr. Smithering needed.

"How is Jerry coming along with Mr. Newley's new horses?" Zeke asked.

"Fine," Mr. Smithering said. "These are some really nice animals. He already has one that can be rode. It didn't take Jerry but a week working with that horse. I don't know how he does it but he can take the wildest horse and in a week, have it meek as a little kitten All he does is talk to them and pet them. It beats anything I've ever seen! I sure can't do it, neither can Mr. Newley."

"Ain't people who can do that called "Horse Whisperers"?" Slim asked.

"Yeah, I've heard of people called that," Zeke said.

"Well, Mr. Smithering, I've got your groceries all fixed up. Here is your bill. Will you be able to carry all them bags to your truck?" "Pee Wee" asked.

Mr. Smithering paid his bill and picked up a couple of bags of groceries.

"Zeke, would you grab a couple of bags and carry then to the truck for me? Thenk you "Pee Wee". See you fellows later," Mr Smithering said

"Thank you and come back to see us," "Pee Wee" said.

Zeke came back inside after taking the groceries to the truck.

"You know, that Smithering boy is really something," Zeke said. "Not many folks can do what that boy can, with horses. I've heard that is the way the Indians trained their horses. I've seen horses that had been trained that way and they really are fine animals."

"Can you see Mr. Newley with anything but the best? "Pee Wee" said. "I'll bet he pays that boy good money. If he don't, he sure ought too. He has trained some mighty fine horses for him. They bring in big money when he sells one of them. A year or two ago a man from Kentucky come down here and bought one of Newley's mares. He sure paid a big price for her."

"Let's all go down there one day and watch him work with the horses," Slim said.

"Let me know about a day ahead ," "Pee Wee" said, "and I'll get my wife to watch the store for a while and I'll go with you."

About that time, two young men entered the store. One of them asked, "Can any of you men tell us where we can find an ole cuss by the name of "Pee Wee"?"

"Boys, I didn't know you was going to be home today!" "Pee Wee" said hugging both of them at the same time. "Have you seen your Mama yet?"

"No, Dad," Jim said. "We thought we'd surprise you both, this time."

"We thought we'd stop by on our way here before we went on to the house to see Mama," Tom said.

"Wait till I run these fellers off and I'll close the store and go with you. It's not long till I'd close anyway," "Pee Wee" said.

Zeke said, "Let's go boys. "Pee Wee" don't need no more money today. It sure is good to see you boys home again." He shook hands with the boys as he was on his way out.

Slim said, "It is good to have you home. Maybe you can keep "Pee Wee" out of trouble for a while." He also shook hands with the boys as he left.

The rest of the men did the same as they went out the door one by one.

"Things never change around here, do they, Dad?" Tom asked.

"Not too much. Good friends are still around. Those men are some of the best friends a fellow could ask for. "Pee Wee" said. "A few things have changed but I'll tell you about all of that later."

"Pee Wee" went to the ice box took out some cokes, stuck them in a paper bag and went to turn the lights off. After he had checked everything and taken the money out of the cash drawer and put it in a paper bag, he followed his sons out the door, and locked it behind him.

"Pee Wee" drove up to his house before the boys did. He got out and went into the house.

"What are you doing home so early?" Easter asked. "Are you sick?" About that time the boy walked in the door.

"Lord, have mercy! Look who is here! Mama's boys are home," Ester said, as she grabbed each boy and gave them a hug and a kiss.

"Just like old times, ain't it, Mama?" "Pee Wee" asked. "Our sons back home again. It sure feels good to have you both home. Let's set down and catch up on things."

"Are you hungry?" Ester asked.

Both boys laughed and gave their Mom a hug.

"You never change, Mom," Jim said.

"And aren't we glad that she doesn't?" Tom asked.

"Home, Sweet, Home," both boys said in unison.

It was late that night when the Billings family went to bed.

Chapter 9

John Peters was still at the Boarding House and still keeping his same routine.

Lucy was still as curious as ever about Peters and still waiting to get her chance to try to sneak into his room and uncover his secret.

Everything in Newleyville seemed to be going smoothly. "PeeWee"'s grocery store was one of the busiest places in town. The men who gathered at the grocery store kept up with all of the happenings in town. They always knew what everybody in town was doing and where they went. That is everyone except John Peters. He still remained a mystery to them. They didn't know anything about him. None knew where he was from or where he went on his daily walks. He talked to nobody in town so they couldn't find out anything about him. This troubled the men at the grocery store.

The men devised a plan to find out were Peters went on his walks. They decided that one of them would leave the store about five or ten minutes, after he had passed by and follow him to see where he went.

Slim was selected to be the first one, then they would take turns after that

They watched the first day for him to pass the store. It wasn't long before Peters came by. After he had gone around the curve in the road, Slim started to walk in the same direction. Slim stayed a distance behind him so that he remained out of sight.

They hadn't gone very far until Slim lost sight of Peters. He started to walk a little faster but he never could see Peters. He had lost him! Slim walked about a mile down the road without any sign of him. Finally Slim gave up and and started back to the store. He heard a truck coming up the road and as it came up to him it stopped. It was Mr. Newley.

He said, "Slim, what are you doing in this part of the country? Would you like a ride? I'm going to the store to pick up a few things."

Slim said, "I just decided to stretch my legs, this morning. I'm a little stiff this morning and I thought I could walk the stiffness out, but I'll ride to the store with you."

He got into Mr. Newley's truck and they continued on to the store. When they got there and went in, Slim shook his head at the men.

"Pee Wee" said, "Come on in here, fellows. Mr. Newley, who is this feller you brought with you? He must be new in town. He sure is a scraggy man. Looks like he's half starved."

By this time the men were all laughing.

Mr. Newley said, "Oh, I saw him walking and felt sorry for him and gave him a ride into town, I think he was lost."

"Now, fellows, a man goes for a walk to loosen up his old stiff joints and you give him a fit about it," Slim said, laughing. "It's bad that you missed me so much, but me and all of my wisdom are here now, and it'll take the rest of the day for me to straighten you out."

"O.K.," "Pee Wee" said. "It's time to get down to business. Mr. Newley, what can I do for you this morning?"

"I have a list of things we need. If you would be so kind as to get them together for me," Mr. Newley said.

While "Pee Wee" was gathering the things for Mr. Newley, the men started talking to him about horses.

"How's Jerry doing with the new horses?" Zeke asked.

"They are really beginning to show a lot of promise," Mr. Newley said. "I think we've got a couple of racers. One of them is a two year old that really shows some promise. He's fast as any horse I've ever seen and he's not reached his full potential yet. Jerry is really working him and I'd say by this time next year he'll be the fatest thing on four legs."

The men all said, "Now ain't that something!"

Zeke said, "Wouldn't it be something if we had a champion from Newleyville? Oh! Man! That horse could put us on the map. People would come from everywhere to see that horse!"

"Pee Wee" said, "Your order is ready, Mr. Newley. I'll help you carry this stuff to your truck."

Mr. Newley paid for his groceries and told the men he'd see them later. Then with his arms filled with bags of groceries, he followed "Pee Wee" to his truck. After the groceries were in the truck he told "Pee Wee" that he would see him and got in the truck and drove off.

After "Pee Wee" was back in the store, his two sons walked in.

"What are you boys up to?" "Pee Wee" asked.

"We thought we'd go riding around a little, to see if anything has changed since we were here the last time," Jim said.

Tom said, "We thought we might stop at the Newley farm to see how Jerry is doing. He's grown up now and we haven't seen him in a year or two. He seemed to be growing up to be quiet a nice young man."

Jim said, "Dad, we'll be home by suppertime. Tell Mom, will you? We'll see all of you later."

They walked out the door and headed for Jim's truck, got in and drove off down the road.

"You've got two mighty fine boys there, "Pee Wee", Zeke said.

All of the other men agreed.

"Their Moma and me are really proud of our sons. They've always been good boys. Now, they are good men. What more could a man ask for? I've got a good wife and two good sons . The Good Lord sure has blessed me and my family and that's a fact." "Pee Wee" said.

"Ain't that the truth?" Slim said.

All of the men agreed. It was the quietest it had been in the grocery store for a while, as each man sat lost in his own thoughts.

Chapter 10

One morning "Pee Wee" came to town to open the store. As usual the group of men were waiting for him outside.

"Zeke, when we get inside you put us a pot of coffee on, "Pee Wee" said. "I haven't had my coffee yet because I overslept this morning"

By that time "Pee Wee" had the door unlocked and turned the knob and went in, the men following close behind him.

"Lord have mercy!" "Pee Wee" said. "Fellows, back out the door and don't touch anything. Somebody has broke into the store!"

"Slim, jump in your truck and go to my house and get the boys. They'll know what to do. They can get the Sheriff here and check this out. Now hurry!"

Slim jumped in his truck and in ten minutes or less pulled in the drive at "Pee Wee's" house. He jumped out of the truck and went running to the door. He started to knock on the door when it opened and Jim stood there.

"Slim, what are you doing here?" Jim asked. "Man, what's wrong? You are pale as a ghost. Is Dad alright?"

About that time Tom came to the door, with his Mother right behind him. "What's going on?" he asked.

"Slim, what's happened to "Pee Wee",? Ethel asked, starting to cry.

"Nothing's wrong with "Pee Wee", Ethel," Slim said. "He sent me to get the boys. Last night somebody broke into the store and everything is a mess in there. He needs the boys."

"Mom, Dad is fine. Just pull yourself together," Tom said, holding his Mother in his arms.

"Slim, come in while we get dressed," Jim said. "You can tell Mom about it. We won't be but a minute."

They all went into the house and Ethel and Slim sat down and the boys went to get finish getting dressed.

" "Pee Wee" opened the door," Slim said, "and we all saw the mess. Stuff all over the floor and glass broken out of the showcase."

"Well, we all backed out the door and "Pee Wee" pulled the door to and locked it. Hadn't nobody touched a thing. So maybe the boys can find who done it."

"Thank the Lord, "Pee Wee" wasn't there." Ethel said. "Well, the boys are ready, so you all go on about your business. I'm fine and nobody is hurt. You boys be careful and I love you, both."

The boys each kissed their Mom, told her not to worry and started out to the car.

Tom said. "Jim, you ride with me, and Slim we'll see you at the store in a few minutes."

The boys took off in Tom's truck, with Slim behind them in his truck.

"Who in the world would break into Dad's store?" Jim asked. "We've known everybody in town all of our lives."

Tom said "Dad said something about a stranger in town. Remember when we first got home?"

"Oh, yeah. I'd forgot all about that. Well, we're here. Let's get this show on the road." Jim said.

"Pee Wee" and the men were sitting on the front porch of the store when Tom and Jim pulled up.

"Dad, tell us what happened." Tom said.

"Boys, I unlocked the door to go in the store and when I opened the door, I saw a big mess. I knew somebody had broke in. I backed right back out the door and locked it back. Nothing has been touched since the robber left. I hope he left you plenty to work with," "Pee Wee" said.

Tom said, "Give me the keys and all of you stay out here, except Jim. He knows what to do."

"Jim, do you have your radio with you?"

"It's in the car at the house but don't you have one in your truck?" Jim asked.

"Yeah. Go call the Sheriff and get him here. Since it's Dad's store, I think it's a good idea to have someone who is not connected with the family to over see this. What do you think?" Tom asked.

"Your're right. I'll go get the Sheriff on your truck radio," Jim said.

He went out the door and went to Tom's truck. He turned on the Police radio and called for the Sheriff. It wasn't but a few seconds until the Sheriff answered the call. Jim told the Sheriff who he was and what had happened. The Sheriff told Jim he would be there in about fifteen minutes and to keep everybody out of the store except him and Tom.

"You and Tom go ahead and see if you can find any clues. There should be plenty, unless it was a professional. If it was we may not find much. I'll see you in about twelve minutes now," the Sheriff said and signed off the radio.

Jim went inside the store and told Tom what had been exchanged between him and the Sheriff. He and Tom started checking to see if they could find how the robber had entered the store. They knew he had not entered by the front door.

They checked the back door to see if they had broken in through that way. They checked the lock and it looked like someone had tried to use a screw driver. The door frame had been torn away with something like a crowbar. The wood was splintered and so was a part of the door.

"This is certainly the way they came in," Jim said.

"We'll need to check for fingerprints over everything," Tom said.

"There's one thing we know he didn't get and that's money because Dad removes all the money every night," Jim said.

The men on the front porch saw the Sheriff coming toward the store. He stopped the car directly in front of the store and got out.

" "Pee Wee", say someone broke in the store last night? Do you know what they took? Did they get any money?" the Sheriff asked

"No, I never leave any money here when I close," "Pee Wee" said.

"You men stick around for a while. I"ll need to talk to each of you," the Sheriff said.

He went into the store to join Tom and Jim.

"Boys, have you found anything yet?" the Sheriff asked.

Jim said, "They broke in the back door. Sheriff, do you remember my brother, Tom? He is an F.B.I. agent and has been for several years now. He is with the Office in Washington."

The Sheriff said, "I remember him as a young man in high school but I haven't seen him since then. I know about him and his work though. It's good to see you, again, Tom."

Tom stepped forward and shook hands with the Sheriff. Tom said, "It's good to see you, again too, Sheriff Lane. I remember you but you weren't Sheriff then. I also remember your, son, Billy. What's he doing now?"

"Billy is a Captain with the Police Department in Little Rock, Arkansas. He's been with them for about ten years, now. He married a girl from there and they have two little boys, Billy, 4 years old and Bob two years old. They keep ole' Bill hopping, just as he did me when he was little," the Sheriff said laughing. "O.K. let's get to work."

"This is the way they came in," Tom said. "Looks like he used a crow-bar. Do you want me to check for fingerprints, Sheriff? I keep a kit in my truck, also several pairs of gloves, so we won't contaminate the scene."

The Sheriff said, "That would be great and save us a lot of time. I would have to call my team in and the main one is on vacation this week."

The men got busy and went over the crime scene with a fine toothed comb. At the back of the store they found several footprints. They seemed to be made by two different pairs of shoes. One pair was quiet a bit smaller than the other. So it appeared that two people were involved.

On the inside of the store, sacks of flour had been torn open and scattered over everything. Some glass jars had been smashed and their contents all over the floor.

They dusted for fingerprints and found a lot but they would have to find out if they belong to the robbers or just someone who came into the store.

A lot of drinks were missing along with a lot of cigaretts and tobacco. Boxes of candy, were missing and so were boxes of cookies, a big stick of bologna and a big block of cheese, also several boxes of matches.

After they had collected all of the evidence they could find they told "Pee Wee" and the other men they could come in and start cleaning up the mess.

All of the men told "Pee Wee" they would help him clean everything up and get the store back in order. They all started and before very long everything was back in order.

The Sheriff asked the men some questions and then told them they were free to go but to be careful until they caught the one that did this.

We will find out who did this and they will be punished," the Sheriff said. "Pee Wee", why don't you close up the store for the rest of the day and go home and get some rest? Your sons and I have a lot to do. Don't worry if the boys don't come home for several days. They are going to be busy. They will get to finish their vacations but right now I really need their help."

Chapter 11

Hector Lane had held the office for the last six years. He was the best Sheriff this county had ever had.

He was tenacious and once he got on a case, you might as well give up, because he would get you no matter how long it took. He had solved every case he had ever had.

He was forty seven years old and had a fearless nature. He was a good honest man and had the respect of everybody, honest citizens, and crooks alike. The crooks feared him because they knew that once he got on your trail he'd get you sooner or later.

He questioned everyone in the town. Everyone that is, except John Peters who had suddenly vanished. No one had seen him for about a week.

The Sheriff talked to Mrs. Benson at the Boarding House and asked her about John Peters. She said that the last time she had seen him was a week ago. She said about five o'clock a teenage boy had come by to see John Peters and they had left together. She hadn't seen him since.

Lucy came into the room. She handed the Sheriff a knife and a piece of folded paper. She said, "I found this in Mr. Peters room. I knew he was hiding something. I found this knife and this paper. I think Mr. Peters is a bad man. His picture is on the paper and it says WANTED at the top of the paper."

"Your a very smart girl, Lucy. Thank you. He is a bad man and I will catch him and put him in jail where he belongs," the Sheriff said.

He told Tom and Jim everything he had found out about John Peters.

"He's hiding out in the woods somewhere in the area. You boys know the places around here like the back of your hand. Let's start looking at every place a man could hide for a while."

"I know several places he could hide out in the woods," Jim said. "Tom do you remember that old shack that's up near Willow Creek? We use to play up there. Remember where I"m talking about?"

"Yeah," Tom said. "I had forgotten that place, but now I remember it. That would be the perfect place to hide out for a while. Sheriff let me get some more agents in on this. This Peters is on the F.B.I.'s Wanted list. It'll take a couple of days for them to get here. This is one really dangerous man. He'd have the three of us dead before we knew what hit us. For this one we need a lot of man power. What do you say?"

"Get you men down here, son. We'll take all the help we can get," the Sheriff said.

Tom went to his truck and immediately put in a radio call to Memphis. He explained the situation to his supervisor and was told six men would be there the next day.

Right after he got off the radio he went to talk to the Sheriff about what he had found out.

Jim said, "Let's go to Mom and Dad's house, get some food and some rest. We're going to need it. Come on Sheriff. You can follow Tom and me in Tom's truck. It's only about ten minutes from here."

"If you think it's O,K. with your folks. I'm ready," the Sheriff said.

As they pulled up at "Pee Wee's" house both "Pee Wee" and Ester came out of the front door to meet them. As they came up the steps to the porch the boys both gave their Mom and Dad a hug.

Jim said, "Mom, this is Sheriff Hector Lane. He's a hungry, tired, man, who needs food and rest just as Tom and I do. We told him to come home with us. We knew he would be welcome."

"It's nice to meet you, Mrs. Billings," the Sheriff said. "I appreciate you taking me in. I've already talked to " "Pee Wee" and as you know Jim and I work together."

"You're always welcome here," Ester said. ""The boys have always brought their friends here. When they were living here, we always had a houseful of boys. All of them called me "Mom" or "Mama" just like the boys did. They still come by to see "Mama" and I'm happy to see them. Now, you all come on in. I just put the food on the table. I'll set three more plates and we'll eat."

They all went inside and straight to the kitchen. While the men washed up for supper, Ester set out their plates and silver ware.

"I made a big pot of coffee if you boys want that, or I've got ice tea," Ester said. "I know "Pee Wee" and the boys want coffee. Sheriff what do you drink?"

"Coffee is fine for me too," he said.

They all sat down at the table and after "Pee Wee" said the blessing, they began to eat.

Ester had cooked a pot roast with carrots, potatoes, onions and cabbage. She had made cornbread and a big coconut cake. They all ate until they were full.

They sat at the table and talked for a while. Then Ester cleared the table, poured more coffee and did the dishes. They got to talking about new people in the community.

"Pee Wee" said, "You know there is a new family that I had forgot about. Do you boys remember where the Burtons used live? Well, about six months or so ago, this new family moved in there, the Russel family. The man's name is Burt. I don't remeber what his wife's name is, but they've got four children, three boys and a girl. The oldest boy is 21, his name is Tim. Then there's a boy Greg, he's around seventeen. Then there's a boy about twelve and I don't remember his name and a little girl about four."

"They've been in the store four or five times, just the man and the two oldest boys. They are pretty rough looking. The boys were all over the store, looking at everything. Now, I don't know what they're like or how they live but I sure didn't trust them two boys. It might not hurt to see what you can find out."

"Dad, who was the strange man you told me about the other day?" Tom asked.

"Oh that's John Peters," "PeeWee" said. "He lives at the Boarding House but I ain't seen him for about two weeks now."

"Well, fellows, I don't know about you but I need some rest," Jim said. "Sheriff, I've got twin beds in my room and you can bunk with me."

"That sounds good to me," the Sheriff said.

Tom said, "You all go ahead to bed. I want to talk to Dad and Mom before I hit the hay. See you in the morning."

Jim and the Sheriff went on to Jim's room and went to bed. They were both asleep in five minutes.

Tom and his parents sat at the table and talked for about half an hour. Then, they too, went to bed. It had been a long day.

Chapter 12

"Pee Wee" opened the store the next day. The men all came as usual. Jim, Tom and the Sheriff were waiting just up the road from the store. They had given "Pee Wee" a coded message to give to the six men who would come in the store later in the morning.

About ten o'clock that morning six men came into the store. They all got a coke and a candy bar. Then they stayed in the store to drink the drinks.

"Where are you fellows from?" Zeke asked.

"We all work in East Tennessee," one of them said.

"We came here because we heard there was a rich iron ore vein somewhere in this area. Some samples had been sent in to the office years ago. The machinery hadn't been invented then to detct the richness of the ore. Now it has, and it's the richest iron ore ever discovered. We're here to check it out. Do any of you have any idea of where we might look?"

""PeeWee" said, "I have an idea. Why don't you go up that road for about a mile? There's a dirt road that turns right, take that road about a hundred yard. Try looking there."

"Thank you, sir. We have to start somewhere. That sounds as good as any. See you fellows later," the man who had done the talking said.

The men left the store and drove up the road. After going about a mile they saw Tom's truck. They pulled over and stopped.

"Tom, have you found out anything yet?" one of the men asked.

"No, we have some clues but we haven't looked for Peters yet. We needed a lot more man power before we go after him. He is really a dangerous man. It will take all of us, and then some, to get him," Tom said.

"There is a family I would like for you to check out," the Sheriff said. "It's the Russel family."

"Now, they don't know Tom or Jim, either one, so one or both of them can go with you to show you where the place is. The two oldest boys could be the ones who broke into "Pee Wee's" store."

Newton, the agent in charge, said, "We have to start somewhere and that sounds like a good place. Let's go boys."

The three of them got into the car and took off to check out the Russel family.

The other five agents were there with the Sheriff. They were trying to decide which direction to start in.

"Men, we could check out the woods around here to see if we could find any clues, as to where Peters is hiding," the Sheriff said. "We won't try to bring him in, just get an idea of where he might be."

"That's a great idea" one of the agents said. "That would give us a head start. We'll have to be as quiet as we possible can, because as smart as he is, he will be watching and he could have booby traps set all around where he is hiding."

"That is exactly the way this should be handled," one of the other agents said. "In fact I don't see how else it could be handled."

"Peters must not find out in any way that we are looking for him," the Sheriff said. "I'm keeping out of town, because someone might say something that Peters would overhear and that would be the end of it."

"By the way where are you staying? the agent asked.

"I'm at "Pee Wee's" house," the Sheriff said. "Neither of them will say a word. They have two sons in Law Enforcement so they know how to keep quiet."

About two hours later Tom, Jim and Tim Newton came back into town. They stopped at the store. They got out of the car and went into the store. Nobody was in the store except the men who were usually there. Jim told them he needed to talk to them about something. He trusted the men completely.

"Men we need your help. We need you to not tell anyone , not even your wives, about what is going on. It could cause a lot of people to be hurt or killed if it got out. Do we have your word that you will not tell anyone?" Jim asked.

"Yes, we won't say one word," the men all said.

Tom said, "This man is an F.B.I. Agent from Washington. His name is Tim Newton. He is head of this investigation. There are five more agents in town."

Tim Newton said, "You won't see them and you won't see much of me but we all will be around very close. You'll see Tom and Jim and you will be able to talk to them if you learn anything. We thank you very much for your cooperation. Good day, gentlemen." He walked out of the store.

Jim said, "Tom, you and I need to get to your truck and go on home."

"You're right," Tom said. "Dad we'll see you at home later. You be careful coming home. Stop for no one or nothing. Come straight home. You men stay with him until he locks up and is on his way home. All of you be careful. Good night."

"What did you think about the Russel family, Tom?" Jim asked.

"If they didn't do the break-in, and I think they did, they are sure guiltly of something." Tom answered. "As soon as Tim hears from the office about the fingerprints, we'll know for sure. It was clever the way he got the boys prints, by handing them his lighter. We got both of the boys prints from that."

The boys went on home and it wasn't long before "Pee Wee" came in. They had supper not long after that.

After supper, they told their parents about what they had found out from the Russel family. While they were talking, there was a knock on the door. Both boys got up from the table, drew their guns and went to the door. It was the Sheriff, so they put their guns away and let him in.

"I'm sorry to be so late getting here," the Sheriff said. "We've been looking around in the woods today. I'll tell you all about it later."

Ester came into the room and said "Sheriff, wash up and I'll get your supper on the table. I know you are hungry as a bear. You can talk while you eat."

The Sheriff washed up and went in to eat supper.

Ester poured everybody another cup of coffee and sat down at the table while the Sheriff ate.

After he finished eating he told Ester how much he enjoyed the meal.

"Well, what did you boys find out today?" the Sheriff asked.

"We went to see the Russel family and we found them," Tom said. "We sat down and talked to them for a while. The man and his wife are not the kind of people who break in stores or any where else. They are as poor as they can be. They are having a really rough time."

"The man lost his job and their home," Jim said. "He has four children and his wife. He hasn't been able to find another job and they're down to their last five dollars. It's a pitiful case."

Tom said, "Those two oldest boys are not the kind to hold a job of any kind. They are plain lazy, good for nothing, boys. I"m sure they are the ones who broke into the store. We got their fingerprints, so it's a matter of matching their prints to the ones we found in the store, and we've got them."

"They are not the smartest boys you've ever met," Jim said. "They think they've got away with it. They didn't have a clue as to what we were really there for. They thought we were really lost."

The Sherif said, "Let me tell you what the agents and I did today. We all decided we'd try to find out where Peters was hiding out. We didn't want him to know we were looking for him, so we decided to be as quiet as possible."

"We entered the woods at the place you parked this morning. We split into three groups, two to a group and started out. We were not very far from each other. I was in the middle group, and we all started at the same time. Well, we got to the top of the hill and started across the ridge to the right. We hadn't gone very far until the agent with me froze and put up his hand for the rest of the groups to stop. He pointed down to his foot and right in front of his foot was a diamond back rattlesnake. I slipped, a step at a time until I was directly behind him."

"The snake was coiled and ready to strike. He knew that if he moved the snake would strike. I whispered to him to jump as far as he could to the side, while I slowly bent down and picked up a small rock. I told him I would throw it on the opposite side of way he jumped. That way the snake would be distracted and strike at the rock. I told him to move his head to indicate the direction he would jump. He nodded his head to the right. I said "Now!" and he jumped just as the rock hit left of the snake and it struck at the rock. We got away from there at a dead run."

"You were afraid to shoot the snake because you knew if Peters was in the vicinity he would hear the shot," Tom said.

"We couldn't shout for that reason," The sheriff said. "Needless to say that ended our search for today. It wasn't a total loss though . One of the agents saw some tracks that were leading in that direction we were heading. They were about the size of the shoes that Peters would wear. Tomorrow we wear boots and go back."

Chapter 13

When "Pee Wee" opened his store the next morning, right after he got in the door Jethro Smithering came in. He was all excited and said, "Pee Wee", have you heard about someone stealing one of Mr. Newley, best horses?"

"No, when did that happen?" "Pee Wee"asked.

"Last night or early this morning," Jethro said. "He came to our house around three O'clock this morning, he asked me and Jerry how the horse was when we left the evening before. He also asked if Jerry had moved the horse to another pasture. Jerry told him he had put the horse in his stall just as he always did before he left for home."

"We went to the farm with him, and we've been searching every pasture and every inch of that farm since three O'çlock this morning. Somebody had to take that horse out of his stall. Mr. Newley has gone to see the Sheriff."

About that time Mr. Newley came in the door at the store.

"Mr. Newley, I'm sorry about your horse,""Pee Wee" said. "Do you have any idea who would do something like that?"

"No, "Pee Wee", I wish I did," Mr. newley said. "I've been to the Sheriff's office and one of the officers told me that he thought the Sheriff was coming to visit your sons, who were home on vacation. Today is the Sheriff's day off."

"Zeke, will you watch the store for me for a while? I'll run to the house and see if he's there. Mr. Newley, if you'll wait, I'll be back in about twenty minutes," "Pee Wee" said.

"I'll wait," Mr. Newley said.

"Pee Wee" got in his truck and started toward his house. "Pee Wee" knew the Sheriff was there, if he could catch him before he and the boys left on their search. In less than ten minutes"PeeWee"pulled into his driveway. He was relieved to see all of the vehicles were still there. He jumped out of his truck and went running into the house. The Sheriff and the boys were having their second cup of coffee.

"Pee Wee" told them what had happened and that Mr. Newley was looking for the Sheriff. He also told them what the officer had told Mr. Newley.

"Well, boys, let's go. It's my job and I've got to check it out," the Sheriff said.

They all headed back to the store.

The Sheriff followed "Pee Wee" into the store. "Pee Wee" introduced the Sheriff and Mr. Newley.

The Sheriff said, ""Pee Wee" tells me that you have some trouble at your farm. Let's go see what we can do about it."

The Sheriff, Tom and Jim followed Mr. Newley to his farm. Jethro was in his truck behind them.

They arrived at the Newley farm and immediately went to the barn to check the stable to see if they could find a clue.

The Sheriff said, "Mr. Newley, is there a way Jim and Tom can take their truck and check out the pastures?"

"Sure," Mr. Newley said, "Just go through the gate beside the barn and there is a gate that leads from one pasture to the other. At the back of each pasture is a pond, just be careful and don't drive in one of those. They're deep and mud is at the bottom."

Jim and Tom went to check out the pastures while the Sheriff was busy at the barn.

They drove through the first pasture, by the pond, without seeing any trace of anything.

They went through the first gate into the second pasture and decided to go by the pond first, then check the other side on their way back. They drove for a while without seeing anything, but as they drew nearer the pond they thought they could see something beside the pond. As they got even closer they could tell it was a horse but it was on the ground. They pulled up to the pond and stopped. It was a horse and it had been shot in the head with what they thought was probably a rifle. It was dead and had been dead for several hours.

They immediately went back to the barn to tell Mr. Newley and the Sheriff.

As they got out of the truck at the barn, the Sheriff said, "That didn't take you boys long. Did you find anything?"

"Yes sir," Tom said, "but I'm afraid it isn't good news. We found the horse by the second pond but it's dead. Somebody shot it in the head, with what appears to be a rifle shot. I'm sorry, Mr. Newley."

"Why on earth would anyone want to kill my horse?" Mr. Newley asked. "I've searched for years for a horse like that and then someone kills it! Why?"

"Some people don't have a reason," Jim said. "They kill for the pleasure of killing. Life has no meaning to them. I'm sorry but that's true."

"Jim is right." the Sheriff said. "Some people are just low down mean and will do anything."

"Jethro, have you seen Jerry this morning?" Mr. Newley asked. "He will be hurt over this. He had worked so hard and acomplished so much with that horse. He loved it so much, if not more, than I did. We had us a winner."

"No sir, Jethro said. "He hadn't come to eat breakfast when I left. I sure hate to tell him about this. He sure was proud of his work with that horse and he did love it."

About that time they saw Jerry coming up the road. He was walking. Just as he got to the gate to the barn yard, they heard a shot and Jerry fell.

They all went running to where he had fallen. Blood was coming from his shoulder. The Sheriff knelt down beside him and checked his heart and the pulse in his neck.

"He's alive but we've got to get him to a doctor in a hurry. Jethro we'll put him in your truck and you get him to a doctor as fast as that truck will go," the Sheriff said.

Mr. Newley said, "Put him in my truck and Jethro can take care of him and I'll drive."

They put Jerry in the back of Mr. Newley's truck and Jethro put his head in his lap. Mr. Newley got in and they started to the doctor. Mr. Newley was really moving when he left the farm and soon he was out of sight.

Tom said, "That shot came from the top of that hill over there. Who ever was doing the shooting really knows how to handle a gun. He didn't mean to kill him or he would have aimed for his head, and he didn't. He hit him just where he intended to.

"There's no point looking for him because he's long gone. That was a person who has done this before and knows what he's doing and how to get away," the Sheriff said. "Boys, let's head back to town and see if we can find the other agents."

Back at the store, "Pee Wee" and the other men had seen Mr. Newley's truck come through town and he was really driving fast. They also saw Jethro in the back of the truck. They knew something was wrong.

"I sure hope the boys are O.K., "Pee Wee" said.

"They are," Zeke said. They just pulled up with the Sheriff."

The three men came into the store. Nobody but the men who were usually there were in the store.

"What has happened?" "Pee Wee" asked.

"The horse is dead and Jerry got shot," Jim said. "He's on his way to the doctor now. We think he'll be O.K."

Tom asked, "Dad, do you know where the men are?"

"No, son, I haven't seen any of them today." "PeeWee" answered.

"They're working and you won't see them unless they want you to," Tom said.

"Did Tim hear anything from Washington?" the Sheriff asked.

"He got some paper this morning, Ester said and then he took off. He left a message for you. He said to tell you that you all are on the right track," "Pee Wee" said.

"They've gone after Peters," Tom said. "There is no telling where they are."

"I have an idea," Jim said. "Tom, remember that place I was talking to you about the other day.? I'll bet you money that is where we'll find him. Let's go check it out. We'll go in a different direction from where the men are going. That way we'll have both sides covered."

"Yeah, I know where you mean," Tom said. "There is another way we can get there and quicker than they can. They have a head start but we'll really have to be quiet. Why don't you and the Sheriff go on that way and remember the other entrance we found one time? I'll come in that way and we'll have our rat caught in a trap he can't escape from."

"I'd forgotten about that place," Jim said. "O.K. Brother, let's go catch us a rat!"

Chapter 14

In the meanwhile Mr. Newley had arrived at the hospital in the town about twenty miles from Newleyville. The doctor had taken Jerry into the emergency room. He had lost a lot of blood and they had to get him stable before they could take him to the operating room to remove the bullet.

Finally they got Jerry stable enough to carry him to the operating room to remove the bullet.

Mr. Newley and Jethro were in the waiting room. The doctors had told them that they didn't know how long he would be in surgery. They would have to wait until they got in there and see how much damage the bullet had done.

Two hours had passed and still no word from the doctors. Three hours passed and no word. Finally after five hours of waiting the doctor came in to talk with them.

He told them that the bullet had entered into the socket of the shoulder, chipping off a piece of bone and then traveled on to lodge under Jerry's collarbone. They had removed the bullet but it had damaged the tendons. They had repaired the tendons and removed the bone chips but it would take a while for it to heal and they didn't know if he would be able to use it as well as he had before. They were going to keep him in the hospital for two or three days to make sure that there was no infection. Jerry had lost a lot of blood and they were going to give him a tranfusion in just a little while. They would keep a nurse with him all night. The doctor said that he also was staying there, in case he was needed.

Jethro told Mr. Newley to go on home and asked if he would tell Jerry's Mother and sister what had happened . He said that Jenny could drive up the next day. She could drive his truck. Mr. Newley said he would do that and that he would also be back the next day

Jethro got to go see Jerry for a few minutes. The doctor assured him that Jerry would be O.K., if no infection set in. They said they were giving him medicine to keep infection down, through his IV. They gave him two pints of blood that night.

The next morning when they let Jethro see Jerry, he was awake. He was in pain and they gave him medication for that. His arm was bandaged to his body so he could not move it and his shoulder was bandaged almost to his neck. The doctors said he was stronger and so far no sign of infection.

About ten O'çlock that morning Jenny, her Mother and Mr. Newley came to the hospital. They got to see Jerry for a few minutes. Later the doctors told them that if no infection showed up today, he could go home tomorrow.

Later that day they gave Jerry some liquids. That night they gave him a light supper. He was doing much better.

Mr. Newley, Jenny and her Mother went home. Jethro stayed with Jerry to bring him home in the morning.

Jerry did well that night and had no infection. Later in the morning after the doctor had seen him, they let him go home. He had to come back in a week to see the doctor.

They stopped by the store to get Jerry a coke. He stayed in the truck and all of the men at the store came to the truck to see him. They were all so glad to see him. In a few minutes Jethro came out and brought the coke and gave it to Jerry.

"We'd better get you on home before your Mother gets to worring, or that arm gets to hurting you," Jethro said. "We'll see you boys later."

They went home. When they got there, Jethro helped Jerry into the house. He and his wife got Jerry in bed and gave him his pain medication. In a little while he was asleep. They closed the door to his room and went into the kitchen to have some coffee. They sat down at the table and Mrs. Smithering asked, "Did Jerry ever ask about the horse?"

"He never has mentioned the horse to me at all," Jethro said. "I know he must have wondered about it, but he has never even mentioned it. Don't say anything about it to him unless he asks you about it. We won't lie to him. Just tell him as little as you can. We don't want him upset."

"We almost lost our son. When I think about that it scares me to death. Why would anyone want to hurt that boy? He has never done anything to anybody and they just shot him down," Mrs. Smithering said.

"I don't know, honey," Jethro said. "The Sheriff will find out who did this to our boy and put them in jail. What worries me, is, will they try it again when he is able to be out? Will they try to hurt Jenny? Will they try to hurt me or you? We don't know who to watch out for because we don't know who did this. It could be anybody," Jethro said.

"We'll just stay home and not get out and we'll keep the kids home to," Mrs. Smithering said.

Jethro said, "Now, honey, you know we can't live like that. I have to make a living. We can't hide for the rest of our lives. I know you're scared but we can't stop living bacause of this. We have to go on living."

"I'm just scared," Mrs. Smithering said. "When you don't know who to fear, you fear everybody. That person could be standing right next to our son and he wouldn't know it . I just want them to catch whoever it is, so our children are safe, again."

"I know, honey," Jethro said. "I won't leave Jerry's side, when he's able to get out, again. Now, don't you worry yourself to death about this. You will only make yourself sick. Our son and daughter are alive and safe. That's what really matters. I hear Jerry calling you. I'll bet he wants some of his Mama's cooking."

Mrs. Smithering went to see what her son wanted. Jerry said, "Mama, I think I'll sit up for a while, with you and Dad. Have you got any coffee?"

"I'll make you a fresh pot," Mrs. Smithering said, "while your Daddy helps you to the table. Jethro, Jerry wants to get up for a while. He needs you to help him."

"Sure, son," Jethro said, "We'll have some coffee at the kitchen table. It'll help you get stronger, to be up a while."

"When I go to sleep," Jerry said, "I dream it's all happening again."

"I know, son," Jethro said. "That will stop after a while. Don't you worry about it. You're home safe with me and Mama. You'll soon be strong again and good as new."

They sat at the table having their coffee. A close nit family who had almost lost their son.

Chapter 15

Not only did the search for Peters continue but so did the search for the one who had shot Jerry and Newley's horse.

Of course, someone had broken in "Pee Wee"'s store and that person or persons had to be found.

The Sheriff said, "We go for all these years without anything major happening, then we have four big cases all at the same time. It's enough to make a Sheriff want to tear his hair out."

The crowd started laughing. Tom said, "Sheriff, now you know what an F.B.I. agent feels like. Sometimes, we feel as if we meet ourself coming in the door as we are going out."

Jim said, "It will all work out, Sheriff. We have the best the F.B.I. has here to help us. They always get their man. Sometimes it takes them twenty years, but they get him."

Tim, the head agent, said, "Tom, your little brother, just almost got in a lot of trouble, talking about that twenty year thing. I had to hold all of these agents off, just to save his life."

They all laughed at that and Tim said, "Aw shucks! Fellows I was just a fooling."

Then they really thought that was funny.

"Men, let's get to moving," the Sheriff said. "These people are not going to turn themselves in. They're waiting for us to come and get them."

Jim, started to the place he had talked to Tom about the other day.

Tom, went up through the woods in the direction that Peters took.

The Sheriff and several of the agents took the trail they had taken before. They all knew Peters was an extremly dangerous man and they would have to surprise him. If they didn't, people were going to be hurt or killed.

Slowly, each group made their way to where the shack was located.

Jim, reached the opening to the cave hidden on the steep hillside. He crawled inside and stood up. He very slowly moved farther into the cave, keeping in the shadows on the side. He smelled coffee and knew they had found their man or somebody. He got close enough he could hear people talking. He couldn't understand what they were saying, so he inched a little closer until he could understand and he stopped. Now, he had to wait for the others to get there.

Tom was just outside the shack when he saw the other agents and the Sheriff come over the ridge. He waited for them to get close, then he went to meet them."We will have to very quietly enter the shack. The opening to the hideout is right behind the shack but the least noise will alert Peters," Tom said. "Jim is already inside. He came in the back entrance. We'll enter one by one and when we reach the entrance we'll storm in together."

Tom entered first and without a sound, went through the back. He stopped at the door of the cave.

In a few seconds the Sheriff slipped through the back and stopped by Tom. Then one by one the agents slipped through until they were all outside the door to the cave.

Inside the cave, Jim stood in the shadows listening to the three people talking.

"Did you ever see the man you were looking for?" the old woman asked.

"No, I've watched for him but I've missed him every time. I heard a shot the other day when I was out and I came back. I thought someone could be looking for me. I don't know who it was or what they were shooting at," Peters said.

About that time a group of men came bursting through the front door of the cave. They had their guns drawn and were pointing them at Peters.

The old woman started to run toward the back of the cave, when Jim walked out with his gun drawn. The woman stopped immediately.

"This is the F.B.I. and you are under arrest John Peters," said Tim the agent in charge.

The Sheriff showed his badge and introduced himself.

"Mr. and Mrs. Peters, you are under arrest for aiding and abedding a wanted criminal," the Sheriff said.

John Peters and his parents were handcuffed and taken out of the cave. After they came out of the woods, the cars and truck were at the road. The prisoners were placed in the Sheriff's car to be taken to jail.

Jim told the Sheriff what he had overheard in the cave.

Jim said, "Peters didn't shoot Jerry. We've still got a lot of work to do."

"I have to get these three to jail," the Sheriff said. "I'll get them booked and get a schedule set up for the men to guard them. I don't want Peters to escape. I'll take a couple of the agents with me, to make sure I get there safely. That is, if it's agreeable with Tim. I'll be back in the morning and we'll continue the work here."

Tim agreed for three of his agents to accompany the Sheriff to carry the prisoners to jail. One man would ride with the Sheriff, while one would ride in front of the Sheriff's car and the other would be behind the Sheriff's car. They would take no chances on Peters getting away.

After the Sheriff got to question Peters he learned what the plan was that Peters had intended to carry out.

Peters had planned, with the help of his parents, to kidnap Mr. Newley's wife and hold her for ransome. He had heard that Mr. Newley was a very wealthy man and very much in love with his wife. If they could kidnap her, he would pay as much money as they asked. Of course they had no intention of keeping her alive. They just wanted the money.

What they got was just another charge.

Chapter 16

The Sheriff got his prisoners in their cells and the roster of officers to guard them.

He took the two agents home with him to spend the night. Tomorrow morning they would be going back to Newleyville to try to solve the other cases.

The Sheriff pulled into his driveway with the two agents. They had left their trucks at the jail and would get them in the morning. They got out of the car and went into the house.

Mrs. Lane was sitting on the couch watching T.V. When the men came in she got up and went to her husband.

She said, "It's good to have you home, honey. I see you brought guests home with you, and if I know you, and I do, you are a hungry man. I'll bet these two men could eat something too. I didn't cook supper, because I didn't know when you'd be in, but I can whip up some ham sandwiches and coffee."

"Honey, these men are F.B.I. agents that I'm working with. This one is Newt and this is Harry. Boys, I guess you have figured out already that this is Hattie, my wife," the Sheriff said.

The men shook hands with Hattie, and Harry said, "Mrs. Lane, it's nice of you to have us here on such short notice. We really appreciate it."

"No trouble at all," Hattie said. "I'll get the food ready. Please, just make yourselves at home. The food will be ready in a few minutes."

The Sheriff said, "Sit down and relax. If your as tired as I am, you're ready to rest for a while. By the way, Jim told me that he overheard Peters tell his parents that he heard a shot the day that Jerry was shot but he didn't see anyone. So, he didn't shoot Jerry."

"That puts a whole new light on things," Harry said.

"Food is on the table," Hattie said. "Come and get it."

A tray of sandwiches was setting on the table, along with a big caramel pie and steaming cups of coffee. The men sat down and began to eat.

After they finished eating Mrs. Lane showed them their rooms. It wasn't but a few minutes until they were ready for bed. After thanking Hattie for a wonderful meal, they retired for the night.

The Sheriff and his wife sat up talking for a while after the agents had gone to bed. He told her everyething that had happened and about the cases they still had to solve.

"Honey, you be careful. These people you're after are dangerous. It doesn't sound like life means much to them. They'd kill you if they got the chance," Hattie said. "I don't want you to get hurt. I know you know what you're doing but I still worry about you. I'm glad that the F.B.I. agents are here plus "Pee Wee's" sons. I know you have the best there is to help you catch these people, but I'll be glad when it's over."

"Hattie, don't worry about me. I will be fine. We are very careful and I have the best of the best, with me. I could not have better crime solvers. We'll find this person or persons and bring them in," the Sheriff said.

"Now, let's get to bed so you will be rested for tomorrow's job. You need to be alert," Hattie said.

The next morning Hattie had got up early and prepared a hearty breakfast for the men. She had country ham, eggs, grits and biscuits, butter and homemade wild blackberry jelly, with steaming cups of hot coffee. The men came in, sat down and ate their fill.

After the agents thanked Hattie for her hospitality and the Sheriff kissed his wife good-by they went on their way back to Newleyville.

They went by the jail and the agents picked up their trucks, then drove on to Newleyville.

They went by "Pee Wee's" store to see if Jim, Tom, and the other agents had already started on their search. They hadn't come by the store so "Pee Wee" assumed that they were still at his house. That is, unless they were searching in the area just above the store. He didn't think that was likely since that direction had already been searched.

"They could have gone to the Russel place to talk with the two Russel boys again," "Pee Wee" said.

"Those boys are connected to this somehow. I don't know how, yet, but my gut feeling says they are," the Sheriff said. "It comes closer to being the store robbery. We're waiting for their prints to come back from Washington. Then we'll know for sure."

Chapter 17

Mr. Newley buried the horse that had been shot. It was buried at the back of the pasture where it had been shot. They put a monument up at its grave. It had never been named but on the monument Mr. Newley had them to inscribe "Jerry's Pride" 1941-1943. It was a beautiful marble stone with a horse's head and then the inscription.

Everyone in town liked Mr. Newley. Although he was a wealthy man, he was also a very generous man. He had helped a lot people during the Depression by carring groceries to families who where having a hard time. He wanted nothing in return and didn't want them to mention it to anyone.

After Jerry got shot, Mr. Newley paid all of his medical expenses. He had been to see Jerry several times since he had been home. One day when he was there, Jerry asked him if they had ever found the horse.

Mr. Newley looked at Jethro and Jethro shook his head. Mr. Newley said, "Jerry you've been to sick for us to tell you before. We did find the horse but someone had killed him. He was shot through the head. We buried him at the back of the pasture. I had a monument put up for him. You know we had never named him but I named him "Jerry's Pride.""

"When you are able to work again, I want you to start working with the other horse. I see a lot of promise in him. I think we could have a winner there. I'm sorry, son, but none of this is your fault."

Jerry sat there with tears streaming down his face. He had never felt about a horse the way he had that one. It touched him that Mr. Newley had called him "Jerry's Pride." He knew he would have been a winner. Maybe he could make a winner out of the other horse but he'd always remember "Jerry's Pride" and what he could have become.

He pulled himself together and thanked Mr. Newley for all he had done for him and his family. He said the doctor said it would be three more weeks before he could go back to work. His arm seemed to be doing fine but they still didn't know how well he would be able to use it.

Jenny was still working for Mrs. Newley. For about the last six months Jenny had noticed a change in Mrs. Newley.

At first Mrs. Newley had been one of the sweetest, kindest people Jenny had ever met. She was a beautiful person, both inside and out. She had long, blond hair and the bluest eyes. She had a very pretty smile and the figure of a model. She seemed to love everybody and everybody loved her.

The first thing that Jenny noticed was that Mrs. Newley, whose first name was Lora, never left the farm. She never went anywhere. Jenny asked her, one time, why she never went with Mr. Newley and Lora told her that she had everything there, so why should she go anywhere?

She would go outside and sit in her rose garden or walk the paths through the other gardens. Sometimes she would even go to the barns with Mr. Newley to see the horses.

Mr. Newley seemed to worship Lora and she seemed to feel the same about him. He always treated her like a queen. He was always bringing her gifts when he came back from being away for a day or two. She had a very beautiful house filled with the most beautiful modern furniture. She had glamorous clothes in the latest fashion. She had diamonds, rubies and pearls.

Jenny noticed that Lora didn't talk much to anyone any more. She spent a lot of time in her bedroom. Sometimes she didn't even come out at meal time. Sometimes she would ask for a tray to be brought to her room, other times she didn't eat at all.

When she came downstairs she would go out and walk out in the pasture or in the woods on the farm. One day she was gone for three hours before she came back.

Some days she didn't even comb her hair and she never wore make up any more.

Jenny had talked to her mother about her because she was worried. Mrs. Smithering told her to talk with Mr. Newley about Lora. She might need to see a doctor. So one day when Mr. Newley came to the house for a little while, Jenny asked him if she could talk to him about something that was bothering her.

The Secret of Jerry's Pride

"Sure, Jenny, what is bothering you?" Do you or your family need anything?" Mr. Newley asked.

"No sir. We're all fine. It's Mrs. Newley, I'm worried about. Do you think she is all right? Is she sick or something? She has not been like herself for several months now. Haven't you noticed it?" Jenny asked.

"Yes, Jenny. I'm worried about Lora, too. She is not herself. I've begged her to see a doctor but she tells me that she's fine and doesn't need a doctor. I know she is not fine. Something is wrong and it is worrying me to death," Mr. Newley said.

"Mr. Newley, I have an idea. What if you could get a doctor to come here? Don't let her know that he is a doctor. Tell her he is a friend of yours who has come to visit for a few days. Let him just be around her for a few days. He could tell if she is sick, and he would know what to do for her," Jenny said.

"That is a great idea, Jenny," said Mr. Newley. "I know just the man. He is a doctor and he is a friend of mine. Lora doesn't know he is a doctor. He took care of my sister before she died. He would do it, too. I'm going to see him today and he'll come if he can. I'll tell Lora I have to go into town and hopefully he'll come back home with me. Can you stay until I get back?"

"Yes, Mr. Newley, I'll be glad to stay. I'll cook your supper for you, so you don't have to worry about it. Maybe I can fix something she'll eat too. She hasn't been eating much lately," Jenny said.

Mr. Newley went upstairs to tell his wife he had to go into town for some things and he'd be back later.

In a few minutes he came back downstairs, told Jenny he would see her later and left the house.

Jenny looked in the cupboard to find something to prepare for supper. She got out several cans of vegetables. Then she went to the basement and got some ham. She also got some potatoes and she carried these things upstairs.

She cooked the ham, green beans, corn, potatoes and made some biscuits. Then she baked a yellow cake with chocolate icing. She also got the coffee ready to make. Then she set the table. She looked around to see if she had forgotten anything. No, everything was perfect.

She heard the front door open and voices. She knew that Mr. Newley was home.

He walked into the kitchen and with him was the most handsome man she had ever seen. He had black hair and very blue eyes with the longest eyelashes she had ever seen. He was tall, dark and handsome.

Mr. Newley said, "Jenny, I would like for you to meet my friend Dr. Steve Standford. Just remember he is Mr. Standford. Steve, this is Jenny Smithering, a neighbor of ours. She helps my wife with the house."

"Jenny, I see that you have our supper all ready."

"Yes sir." Jenny said. "I'll turn on the coffee and put the biscuits in the oven. All you have to do is take them out of the oven when they're brown. Everything else is ready. I'll go on home now but I'll be back in the morning.

"Mr. Standford it was nice meeting you. I hope you can help Mrs. Newley. I'll see you tomorrow, Mr. Newley.

Thank you. Maybe everything will be better now. Good night to you both."

"Good night," the two men said, as Jenny walked out the door.

Chapter 18

The Sheriff and the F.B.I. agents were busy. They had been back to the Russel farm but this time had not gone to the house to talk to the family. They had the farm staked out and were watching the movements of the family.

Several times the two oldest boys had sneaked out of the house after their parents were asleep and gone to some of the other houses and were prowling around them.

Each time this happened three or four of the agents had followed them but so far they had not caught them stealing anything. They seemed to be looking for something that they had not found , so far.

The agents and the Sheriff had split into two different units. One group would watch the place and especially the boys during the day and the other group would take over at night.

Jim and Tom were now in different groups. Jim had contacted his boss in Little Rock and told him all that was going on at home and got an extention on his leave from work until they could catch the criminals.

Of course Tom was on the job with the other agents and his boss knew all about what was going on.

The Peters were still in jail. John was wanted in so many different states until they were having a problem deciding which state would try him first. They had to figure out where his crime spree had started. Several states had found bodies and they were working those cases to see if he had any connection to those murders. One thing was for sure, John Peters would never be a free man again and neither would his parents. Their criminal record streached back over a period of many, many years.

One night, while the Sheriff's group was watching the Russel place, the boys slipped out and they had brought their rifles with them.

The agents followed them as usual but this time, they took their Daddy's truck. They went through Newleyville but did not stop. They went on to the next town and went on through and stopped at a farm just on the other side of town. It was a large house and had several out buildings.

They had stopped about half a mile from the house and had gone on foot the rest of the way. The agents had followed them but stayed behind just farther enough so they would not be seen.

The boys made their way to the house and started going through the barn and then the out building. Each time they came out of a building they had nothing. After they had searched every thing else they went to the house.

They tried the doors and windows at the back. They had started around the house when the dog that was sleeping on the front porch woke up and started barking. The boys took off back around the house and took off for their Daddy's truck. The dog came off the porch and started after them. The boys were fast runners and had a little head start on the dog. It wasn't but a few minutes until they were off the property and the dog turned and went back to his bed on the front porch.

The agents knew the boys were headed back to the truck and they got to their car before the boys got to the truck. When they reached it, they took off for home, with the agents not far behind them.

The men in the car were talking and laughing about how fast those two boys could run when a dog was chasing them. They had never seen two boys who were more scared. They laughed about it all of the way back to the Russel place. They didn't think the boys would go back to that house again.

Tom seemed to think that they would try to rob "Pee Wee's" store again. Since they thought that they had got by without getting caught the first time, they wouldn't be afraid of being caught if they did it again.

The men decided that they would form different groups and try a new stragedy. A small group would continue to watch the Russel place. Then they would follow the boys if they left the house.

Another group would keep the store under survalience. Meanwhile Tom and Jim would hide in the store every night. If they all worked this way the whole group would be at or near the store, in case the boys did try to break in the store again. The boys would be surrounded and they would have them. They decided to let the boys get inside the store before they apperended them.

They told "Pee Wee" of their plan and he agreed. Tom and Jim would slip into the back of the store just before "Pee Wee" closed at night. They could sleep during the day and so could the second crew.

The first crew would also sleep during the day, because the boys had made no attempt to leave the home during the day. Their dad kept them busy all day. They had no chance to leave then, so they knew it would be at night.

Just after it became twilight each group went to their assigned places. Tom and Jim slipped into the store from the back way. Not even the men sitting in the store heard them come in. "Pee Wee" made sure the men were all out of the store before he took the money from the cash register, then he checked on his sons.

Tom said "Now, Dad, you go on and lock up and leave as usual. We do this all the time, so we know what we're doing."

"Dad, don't you and Mom stay up worrying all night," Jim said. "Tom and I are armed and we have two groups backing us up. Nobody will get hurt. Everyone of these men, do this for a living. They are all well trained to do jobs like this all of the time. Good-night, Dad. We'll see you in the morning."

"Pee Wee" went out the door locking it behind him. The boys got settled to wait to see what, if anything, happened.

Everything was quiet for the first part of the night. Then around midnight they heard a noise at the back door. They got out of sight behind the counters, one on each side of the store. They could hear somebody talking just outside of the back door. Who ever it was wasn't trying to be quiet. They had no fear of being caught.

"Dog gone, he's done changed the locks on the door. Hand me the crowbar and I'll pry this door open," one voice said.

"Here, let me get there. I don't think you can pry it open," another voice said.

Then there was a noise of breaking wood. The door opened and two figures walked in the store. They headed to the front of the store.

"Check to see if he left any money in the register. I'll get all of the cigaretts I can carry and put them in the truck and then I'll come back and get some more," one voice said. He grabbed up an armload of cigaretts and took off. In a few minutes he was back.

Jim and Tom slipped from their hiding places and with their guns drawn, walked quietly up behind the two boys.

"Put your hands up! Tom said.

The two boys jumped as if they had been shot.

"Put your hands on top of your head and lace your fingers together," Jim said. "Now back up toward my voice."

The two boys did as they were told. Before they knew what was happening Tom had one handcuffed, while Jim did the same with the other.

The Sheriff and six agents came walking in the back door.

The Sheriff said, "Well, well, boys! Was one time not enough for you? You had to try it again to try to get it right. You are under arrest for breaking and entering, not once but twice. You are also being charged with theft, again not once but twice. Take them to my car, boys and I'll give them a free ride to jail. They'll like it there with the ones who are in there for murder."

Tim turned to the Sheriff and said, "I don't know why the rest of us didn't just go on home and go to bed. Tom and Jim didn't need us. They had those two wild boys under arrest before the boys knew they were any where around."

The Sheriff laughed and said, "I thought those two boys were going to faint when those two tough law men told them to put their hands up. I don't think they would have been more scared if two ghost had jumped out at them."

"All kidding aside, you two did a great job," Tim said.

"You did, slick as a button," the Sheriff said.

"Thank you, gentlemen," Tom said, bowing to the two men.

"We were were glad to show you fellows how to get the job done," Jim said laughing.

"Well, I'll take these two and lock them up. Newleyville is going to fill my jail up. That's two cases solved and that leaves one to go. I won't need an escort for these two," the Sheriff said.

"Tim, we're going to nail this back up, and lock the door back, and we'll be on home. You go on and get some rest," Tom said.

"Sheriff, will you be back in the morning to work on that other case, or do you want to take a day off and let us do some noseing around?" Tim asked.

"You know, if you fellows don't mind I might do that," the Sheriff said. "I've got paper work piled up a mile high on my desk. I'll see you fellows day after tomorrow. Good night."

"The rest of the agents are going to spend the night in the Sheriff's town, but they will be back in the morning," Tim said.

By that time, Tom and Jim had everything secure at the store and were ready to go home and get some rest.

Chapter 19

Dr. Standford had been at the Newley home for two days. He had talked to Mrs. Newley two or three times but it had only been very short conversations.

Lora was coming downstairs now for meals. She had lunch and supper with her husband and Steve yesterday. She seemed a little better than she had been before but she had very little to say to anyone.

"I'm glad you came to visit, Steve," Lora said. "Mr. Newley needs some male companion ship every now and then."

"Thank you, Lora" Steve said. "It's been a while since I've had a vacation, and I can think of no lovelier place to be. You have a most beautiful home and your gardens are supurfine. The roses are the prettiest I've ever seen."

"Thank you," Lora said.

Jenny was now coming to the house every day and prepared all of the meals, except for breakfast . Mr. Newley prepared their breakfast each morning.

"I think I'll sit in the garden for a while, Jenny," Lora said.

Steve said, "Would you like some company?"

"No, thank you. "I'd like to just sit quietly, alone and enjoy the fresh air." Lora said.

After Lora had gone outside and went into the rose garden, Jenny had a chance to talk to Mr. Newley and Dr. Standford.

"Have you found out what is wrong with Mrs. Newley, Dr. Standford?" she asked.

"No, I'm afraid I haven't had much of a chance to talk with her. Although Mr. Newley tells me that her coming downstairs is an improvement," Steve said

"Yes, it is," Jenny said. "That is the first time she has gone to the garden for almost a month. You see, she use to be out there every day. She loves her roses and she would be out there for hours making sure that not one weed was in them."

Mr. Newley said, "My Lora, looks so sad. I miss her beautiful smile. She so seldom smiles any more. It's as if she is away in a far away place where I can't reach her any more. Steve, you must find out what is wrong, so we can make her well again."

"Try not to worry, Newley," Steve said. "It may just be that she is having a case of mild depression. We'll find out what is wrong and make it right again."

About that time Lora came back inside. She said, "Excuse me, dear, I didn't realize we had guests. Who is this lovely couple, dear?"

Jenny's mouth dropped and she looked at Mr. Newley, speechless.

"My dear. this is Steve Standford, an old friend of mine. He is on vacation and came to visit us for a while."

"You know, Jenny, she has been helping you with the house and the cooking. You've been so busy with your roses, so we got Jenny to help us out for a while," Mr. Newley said.

"Yes, yes, of course. I must have forgotten. I seem to forget things so easily these days. Now, where did that child go?" Lora asked?" "Mother, doesn't like for her to be playing in the house, you know."

Steve came over and took her by the arm and said, "Lora, come and sit down for a while and Jenny will fix you a nice cup of tea. "Wouldn't you like that?"

"Why, yes I would if you gentlemen will join me," Lora said.

Jenny made the tea and set the cups on the table. She also put some homemade sugar cookies on a plate and placed them on the table.

Steve went to his doctor's bag and handed Mr. Newley a vile of pills. "One, three times a day" he said. "One, now please."

"Dear, you forgot to take your medicine," Mr. Newley said.

"Yes, I did. Thank you." Lora said taking the pill from Mr. Newley and putting it into her mouth and taking a drink of the tea.

"Would you gentlemen like some cookies?" she asked.

"Now, where did Mother say she was going? Since that Mr. Randolph came here I can't keep up with her comings and goings. I wish he would leave. I don't like him," she said.

"When did Mr. Randolph come?" Steve asked.

"You know, about two months ago. He says he loves Mother, but he doesn't! He loves her money! He isn't good to her, you know. I heard him strike her the other day!" Lora said.

"I think I need to lie down for a while. I am so tired," she said.

"Come with me," Jenny said. I'll turn your bed down and help you get undressed so you can rest."

Jenny put her arm around Mrs. Newley and gently helped her up the stairs.

When they had gone, Steve said, "Newley, I'm afraid Lora is haveing a nervous break down. I think we caught it in time to help her. The medication I gave you will help her rest but I have something else I want to give her twice a day. It should help her come back to reality after a while. Now, she needs the rest. By the way, where is her mother?"

Mr. Newley said, "About three years ago her sister found their mother dead. We all thought the Randolph man, she had married, had something to do with her death but we could never prove it. He died a year later."

Steve said, "That's her problem. She has had that bearing on her mind until her nerves just got the best of her. Don't you worry, we'll make her well again but it will take some time."

Jenny came back downstairs and said, "She's asleep. She looks like she is really resting. She has slept so little lately and when I check on her, even in her sleep, she tosses and turns. I think the rest will do her good. Dr. Standford what is wrong with Mrs. Newley? I've never seen her like that before."

"As I told , Newley, I think she is having a nervous breakdown. He said that her mother was found dead three years ago and they think her husband killed her, but could never prove it. He died before they had the proof. She has had that on her mind and her nerves just couldn't stand up under the stress." Steve said.

"Will she be all right?" Jenny asked.

"Yes, Jenny," Mr. Newley said. "Steve said it would take time but she can recover, We'll have to keep her calm and Steve gave me medicine to give her. She'll also need a lot of rest. Will you look after her, Jenny?"

Without hesitation, Jenny replied, "Mr. Newley, I will do anything I possibly can to help Mrs. Newley. You know how much I think of her. She has always been so good to me."

Jenny finished her chores and went home, leaving Mrs. Newley in the care of Mr. Newley and Dr. Standford.

Chapter 20

The Sheriff, the agents, Jim and Tom went up into the woods where they thought the shot had come from that hit Jerry.

They formed a wide circle and covered every inch of ground looking for the spent cartiage. They covered that ground but found nothing.

This time they went a little higher up the hill and did the same thing again. They were slowly moving down the hill when Jim said, "Stop! I've found something." He moved the leaves and picked up a cartiage shell.

It looks like a long rifle shell for a 22 rifle," Tom said.

Tim and the Sheriff looked at it. Then Tim said, "From this distance it wouldn't be hard to hit somebody where Jerry was standing."

"Did any of you talk to Jerry after he came home?" the Sheriff asked.

"No, I went to see him right after he came home, but it was just to see how he was doing." Jim said.

"So, nobody has talked to him about the shooting." the Sheriff said.

"Today would be a good day to do that, wouldn't it?" Tom asked. "I'll be happy to do it. I haven't seen Jerry in several years now. I'll talk to him."

Tom got in his truck and went to visit Jerry. It didn't take him long to get to the Smithering's house. He pulled up in front of the house and got out of his truck. Jerry and Jethro were sitting on the front porch.

"Come in, Tom," Jethro said. "What are you doing in our neck of the woods?"

"Hello, Jerry, Jethro, How are you two doing? Jerry, you look great. Are you doing O.K. now? You are one lucky man. I'm glad to see you up," Tom said.

"Pull up a chair, Tom," Jerry said. "I haven't seen you in a long time. Are you still with the F.B.I.? That must a great job, but somehow I don't think I would like it much. I'd much rather work with horses than people."

"Speaking of horses, Jerry, on the day that you were shot did you see anyone on the road when you were coming to the Newley's?" Tom asked.

"No, I walked up there that day, because I thought I might see the horse that had run away,," Jerry said. "Of course I didn't see him or anything else."

"Jethro, did you see anyone on the road or on the hill across the road?" Tom asked.

"No, The only person I saw that morning was Mr. Newley and then Jerry," Jethro said.

"Well, who ever was on that hill that morning is the person who shot Jerry. We had thought it was Peters, but he didn't do it. He didn't know anyone had been shot that morning." Tom said. "By the way, Peters is in jail.

You won't see him again because he'll spend the rest of his life behind bars."

"So, you boys caught him," Jethro said. "Where was he?"

"In a cave behind the old shack," Tom said. "He had been living there for a while. He's an extremely dangerous man. I'm glad we caught him before he killed anyone else."

"I figured it was Peters," Jerry said. "I don't know why anybody would want to shoot me. I don't do anything but work with Mr. Newley's horses, and stay at home, when I'm not working."

"Well, I'd better be getting on back. We've got work to do. We'll get the person who shot you, Jerry. I don't know when, but we'll get them," Tom said. "It's a tough case because nobody had a motive, and we have no suspects. We do know you were shot and someone did it. Take care both of you. I'll see you later."

"Thanks for coming by, Tom. It was good to see you, again. You all be careful and don't get hurt," Jerry said.

After Tom left, Jerry and Jethro talked about what he had told them.

Jerry said, "Dad, I've thought about that morning a lot. Do you think it could have been a hunter and it was just an accident?"

"No, Jerry I don't . Who ever shot you was aiming at you. It wasn't no accident. I sure wish it had been," Jethro said.

Tom went back to town to tell the men that Jerry didn't know anything.

The Sheriff said, "Men, tell me what we do now. I don't have a clue. We have a 22 rifle cartiage with no weapon, no suspect, and no motive. The only thing I know to do now, is to start over."

Jim said, "Let's see if we can find the casing near where the horse was shot."

"That would prove the same weapon was used to kill the horse, and shot Jerry," Tom said.

"It's worth a try," Tim said.

The men went to the Newley farrm. Mr. Newley and Dr. Standford were at the barn, checking on the horses. Mr. Newley introduced Dr. Standford to the men. They all shook hands and then the Sheriff told Mr Newley why they were there.

"With your permission we would like to check the grounds around where the horse was shot." the Sheriff said. "What we are looking for is a spent casing from the gun that was used. We found one casing, on the hill across the road, from the gun used to shoot Jerry. We would like to find a casing from the gun used to shoot the horse, to see if the two match."

"Yes, of course, you may look any where you want to," Mr. Newley said. "I hope you find something, because the person who did all of this needs to be caught. They could hurt or kill someone else."

Jim said, "Would you mind showing us where the horse was shot?"

"Sure," Mr. Newley said. "It would be easier if you went in a truck. I think we all can get in one truck."

Tom got in his truck and pulled through the gate at the side of the barn. All of the men got in the truck. Mr.

Newley got in the cab with Tom, so he could show him where to stop.

They arrived at the location and got out. The men commented about the marker and how nice it was. Then they began their search. They spread out quiet a distance from where the horse had fallen. They didn't think it had been shot at close range.

They moved over the area very slowly, because it would be hard to find in the grass. After covering the area to where the horse had fallen, and finding nothing, they turned and went back. They were going to cover the same area again, working outward this time. They had covered almost the whole distance, when one of the agents, near the center of the group, called out, "I've found two empty casings," he said. The other agents went to where he stood. They moved very slowly, looking before they took a step. They hoped to find a casing in case more then two were present. None of them found anything.

"We know at least two shots were fired but only one found its mark," Tim said. "These casings look like they also came from a 22 rifle. After they're put under a miscroscope, we'll know for sure."

"O.K.. Thank you, Mr. Newley," Tim said. "We"ll get this to the lab, so they can check it out for us. Then we'll know for sure if all of the casings came from the same gun. Then we'll go from there."

The men all got back in the truck and went back to the barn. There Mr. Newley and Dr. Sandford got out and the rest of the men went on their way.

Chapter 21

Dr. Standford was still staying at the Newley home taking care of Lora Newley. She seemed to be improving, but very slowly.

There were days that she would be very aware of her surrounding, and talked with Jenny about the usual house hold things. Those days she would go out to her rose garden, and do some weeding and take care of the roses.

Then there were days that she stayed in her room and didn't even come out to have her meals with everyone else.

Some days she came out of her room and came downstairs, but would not really be herself at all. Her mind was in the past, and she relived again her childhood, or the time around her Mother's death. Lately it seemed those times were happening farther and farther apart. Dr. Standford thought that was a good sign that she was beginning to recover.

Jenny really enjoyed the days when Lora seemed to be "herself" again. They would talk as Jenny went about doing her house work. Mrs. Newley would plan the menu for the meals, which Jenny would prepare.

During those days, Lora would join the others at mealtime and carry on a conversation with them.

Sometimes she would even tell a funny event that had happened that day, and the room would be filled with laughter.

Mr. Newley continued giving Lora her medicine every day and Dr. Standford continued to moniter her progress.

One day, after Lora had gone out to her rose garden, he talked to Mr. Newley and Jenny. That had been a good week for Lora and she seemed to be happy.

Dr. Standford said, "If Mrs. Newley can continue the way she is now for a month, then I think she will be recovered. She may slip back a few times before she makes a full recovery, but she is well on her way to a full recovery."

Jenny said, "I can see her improving almost every day. It makes me so happy to see her laughing again, the way she use to."

"My Lora is back on those days," Mr. Newley said. "She sleeps all night now without the nightmares she was having. She awakes in the mornings with a smile and in a cheerful mood. I only hope she stays this way. It breaks my heart when she is so upset and unhappy."

Jerry came up that week for the first time since he had been shot. He and his dad drove up in the truck around seven thirty that morning. Jethro drove up to the gate leading into the barnyard. Jerry got out and Jethro waited at the gate for them to go in together.

Jerrry felt very nervous when he got to the gate, but Jethro walked through with him. Then he closed the gate behind them.

They hurried into the barn. Mr. Newley and Steve Standford were already in the barn feeding the horses.

"Well, look who's here! Jerry, my boy, how are you doing?" Mr. Newley asked. "It's so good to see you. Did the doctor say it was alright for you to come back to work? If you get tired or it's too much too soon-home you go. I want you to meet a friend of mine. He's here visiting for a while. Steve, this is Jerry and his Dad. Jethro is also Jenny's Dad. Fellows, this is Steve Standford."

"It's nice to meet the two of you. I feel as if I already know you. I've heard so much about you," Steve said.

As they shook hands, Jerry said, "Nice to meet you too. We've heard a lot about you from Jenny."

Jethro said, "Nice to meet you, sir. Mr. Newley, Jerry had stayed away from the horses as long as he could stand it. His arm is almost as good as new. It's still a little stiff but the doctor thinks that will get better with time. He's still kind of nervous and his has some nightmares, but he is doing fine. Look at his face. When he's with the horses, he's happy."

Jerry had walked over to the stall of the newest horse. He petted it and started talking to it. The horse acted as if he recognized Jerry and was glad to see him. He rubbed his head against Jerry's shoulder.

Jerry said, "We'll make a winner out of you, won't we boy? You are a winner, I just know it. You're a wonder boy, that's what."

Mr. Newley was standing near-by and said, "Jerry, you just named our horse. "Wonder Boy" sounds good to me and I think he likes it, too."

"You know, I think he does too. Look at him! He knows he's a winner. Don't you boy? We'll make a winner out of him too, Mr. Newley. Just you wait and see. He has the spirit of a winner and the determination, too," Jerry said.

Steve said, "I walked over to that horse the other day and he wouldn't let me get close to him. Jerry walks up and he lets him pet him and then he rubs Jerry's shoulder with his head. If that isn't amazing! That man has magic with horses."

"He's always been that way with horses," Jethro said. "Well, really not with just horses but with all animals. I've seen him calm a mean dog down and it would wind up licking his hand. It' just a gift he was born with because nobody taught him."

"That kind of talent can't be taught," Mr. Newley said. "I've worked with horses all of my life and I certainly can't do it. Jerry is one in a million."

"Steve, do you remember Little Deer, the Indian that lived near our farm, when we were growing up?" Mr. Newley asked."

"I sure do," Steve said. "He had that same kind of talent. Your Dad would get him to come over when he had a horse that nobody else could tame. Remember Boy Blue and how wild he was?"

Mr. Newley said, "Little Deer made him tame as a kitten. I rode that horse for years after that."

Jerry put the bridle on Wonder Boy and led him out in the barnyard. He walked him around, talking to him all of the time and petting his neck. He kept walking the horse for about fifteen minutes.

"Mr. Newley," Jerry called, "Come very slowly up to Wonder Boy. When you get near him, call him. Then just walk up and pat him on his neck while you're still talking to him. Pat his neck for a few minutes, then turn and walk away."

Mr. Newley did as Jerry had asked him. When he got close Wonder Boy kind of shied closer to Jerry.

Jerry said, "It's alright, boy. Easy, easy now. Nothing is going to hurt you."

Mr. Newley kept walking toward the horse and calling his name. He reached out and petted Wonder Boy on the neck, and the horse did not move. He did that for about five minutes, then turned and walked away. The horse never moved. Jerry led him back inside the barn, opened the gate to the pasture, took off the bridle and told the horse to go on out in the pasture. Then he came back and turned the other horses out into the pasture.

"In about an hour, I'll go out and put the bridle on him and work with him some more." Jerry said. "In about a week, I'll ride him. Then I'll teach him to run. He's a winner. I feel it. I think he'll be better than Jerry's Pride. He is smarter and has more spirit."

Chapter 22

The F.B.I. labs had compared the three casings from the shots that had been fired and decided that they all three had been fired from the same gun.

They also checked out the bullet that had been removed from under Jerry's collarbone. They said it was a 22 rifle that had fired that bullet. They had no weapon to check to see if that particular gun had fired the bullet.

The Sheriff and the agents now had to try to locate that 22 rifle. That meant that they would have to check the whole town to try to locate the rifle. Each rifle would have to be fired, the casing labeled and the bullet that had been fired labeled to match the casing. It would take a long time, and then they'd have to wait for all of them to be processed at the lab and the report to come back.

Then they would have to take the rifle that matched the labled bullet and casing and send it in to make sure that bullet and casing had been fired from that rifle.

The men would split into groups of two, except one group would have three in it. There would be three groups.

The men set out to cover the town. One man in each group would put in a notebook the name of the owner of the rifle, number of the casing and bullet from that rifle.

Group one would start with the number one and go as far as they needed. Group two would start with the number one hundred and go as high as needed. The third group would start with the number two hundred and go as high as needed.

After they had mapped out the area each group would cover, they started out.

The first house group one came to was "Pee Wee's" house. They asked Ester if they had any 22 rifles. She said "Yes, we have three. "Pee Wee" had one as did each of the boys."

They took the rifles outside and shot each one into a post. As they shot each one they labled it and dug the bullet out of the post and labled it the same number as the casing. Each name was written in the book and the number that went with it was written beside the name.

That group went from house to house doing the same thing at each house that owned a rifle. Almost all of them did but some owned a shotgun, but no rifles. These were not tested.

Group two had the area in which Zeke lived. Bertha gave the men Zeke's rifle and they shot it and wrote his name and numbered the casing and the bullet just as the first group had done. Then they went on from house to house.

Group three had the Russel's house, the Smithering house and the Newley house in their area, plus the other houses.

They went to the Russel house first. Mr. Russel said they only had one rifle and he gave it to them. They did the same thing the other two groups had done.

Mr. Russel apologized to the men for the robberies his sons had commited.

The Sheriff said, "Mr. Russel, you do not need to apologize for your sons. We know you and your wife did not raise your sons to be that way. You are good, honest, hard working people. Our children do not always follow our examples or our teachings. You are not responsible for that. I'm sorry that your family had to go through that. The boys are young, so maybe this will teach them a lesson they won't forget. Their trial comes up next week. Thank you for your help. We'll see you soon.

The group went on their way from house to house. Then they came to the Smithering house. Mrs. Smithering gave them Jethro and Jerry's rifles. They did the same thing they had done at each house where there was a rifle.

The next house they came to was Mr. Newley's house. They saw him at the barn and told him what they were doing.

"Sure, I have a rifle at the house," Mr. Newley said. "I'll go to the house with you and get it for you."

The men stayed on the porch until Mr. Newley came back out. It seemed it was taking him a while. A little later he came out with the rifle in his hand.

"Gentlemen, I'm sorry it took me so long, but my wife had taken it out of the rifle cabinet and I had to look for it. She had carried it upstairs and put it in her closet. I did find it, so here you are, and I also brought a shell," Mr. Newley said.

The men took the rifle and did the same as they had done at all of the other houses. Then they gave Mr. Newley his rifle back. He carried it back into the house and put it back in the cabinet.

The groups finished their areas and met at "Pee Wee's" store. They took the books and the casings and bullets and checked to make sure they were all correctly matched. Then the casings and the bullets were carefully packed in a box to be sent to the F.B.I. lab to be checked to see if any matched the ones they had found at the scenes of the crimes. The Sheriff would send them to the lab that afternoon.

Now, all they had to do was wait until they heard from the lab in Washington.

The Sheriff took the box and left, telling the men he would see them at the trial on Monday morning.

Chapter 23

The Russell boys trial was to be on Monday, in the courthouse, in the town where the Sheriff lived.

The agents, Tom and Jim were to be witnesses. They arrived at the courthouse around eight thirty that morning.

The court was called to order at exactly nine O'çlock. The Russel, boys along with their attorney were seated at the Defence table. The Prosecutor was seated at the other table. The Judge asked the boys how did they plead?

Both boys said, "Guilty."

So there would be no trial. The Judge gave each of the boys six years in prison for two cases each of breaking and entering and thieft. They were taken to prison that afternoon to begin serving their sentences.

Peters had already been taken to prison, because he had been in prison when he escaped. He also had fifteen cases for bank robbery, fourteen cases of breaking and entering, and thirty two cases of theft. Then ten years had been added on for the escape from prison. He would never be out of prison again. His mother and father were sentenced to house arrest at an old folks home. The doctor said they wouldn't live over six months, because they were both very ill from living in the damp cave for so long. Neither of them could now walk and were confined to wheel chairs but most of the time they were unable to get out of bed.

On their way back to Newleyville, Tom and Jim got to talking about who could have shot Jerry.

"Im at a complete loss," said Jim. "I don't have a clue. We've known these people almost all of our lives. None of these people have ever done anything dishonest in their lives. They would not take a candy bar without paying for it. Who do you think did it, Tom?"

Tom said, "Well, we know who didn't do it. Mr. Newley, Jethro and Jerry were all together at the barn, when it happened. We know Peters didn't because he thought they were shooting at him and he was to far away at the time."

"The Russel boys were no where near the Newley farm when the shooting took place. Who does that leave? Nobody!"

"Yet, Jerry was shot by somebody," Jim said. "We know that. Maybe the F.B.I. lab can give us an answer."

Tom said, "I don't want to leave Mom and Dad here with an attempted murderer on the loose, do you?"

"No, I don't," Jim said.

Chapter 24

Each day Mrs. Newley was getting stronger and her mind was getting better. Dr. Standford seemed to think that if she kept improving as she was now that in three or four months she would have a complete recovery and be back to her usual happy self. Sometimes patients, who have been ill in the same way she had, never had a relapse and lived a full, happy life from that time on until their deaths. Others, however, would slip back and never fully recover.

He said, "It depends on the person. Each case is different and you never really know what the outcome will be. I really think, in Lora's case, with her personality, if we can reach the stage of once getting her back, she will remain well. These cases take time, some more than others."

One day Mr. Newley was talking to Jenny and he asked, "Jenny, what do you think about Steve?"

Jenny said, "Mr. Newley, I think he is a very good doctor and has really helped Mrs. Newley. She seems a lot better to me, than she has in months.

"No," he said. "I mean what do you think about him, as a man?"

"He is a very, nice man," Jenny said. "He is a gentle, careing, person. He has a good sense of humor and seems to be a good doctor."

"Well, I'm afraid that Steve has fallen in love, and he doesn't know what to do about it," Mr. Newley said. "He's even talking about giving up his practice and moving."

"Oh!" Jenny said.

"The young lady he is in love with is a very nice preson. She's kind, gentle and very pretty. I think they would make a wonderful couple." Mr. Newley said. "He has even discussed setting up his practice in her home town because it doesn't have a doctor now."

"I hope he will be happy," Jenny said. Then she hurried out of the room.

Mr. Newley, went back to the front porch and sat down. Steve and Lora were sitting out there having a glass of lemonade.

"Did you ask Jenny to join us?" Lora asked.

"No, my dear," Mr. Newley said. "I think she is preparing our supper. She was setting the table when I went in, so I say we'll be eating in about fifteen minutes."

Jenny began putting the food on the table. Then she went and washed the tear stains from her face and went to call them to tell them supper was ready.

They got up and came into the house. The men went to wash up before they sat down and Jenny was pouring the coffee in the cups.

The men came in and Mr. Newley pulled out Mrs. Newley's chair and she was seated. Steve pulled out Jenny"s chair and she was seated. Then both men were seated.

They filled their plates and were eating. Steve, Lora and Mr. Newley were talking but Jenny was sitting there very quiet. She finished her meal and got up to get the dessert.

She cleared the table and put their dessert on the table. Then she refilled the coffee cups. But instead of sitting down for dessert as she usually did, she started washing up the dishes.

"Jenny, aren't you having dessert with us tonight?" Lora asked.

"No, thank you," Jenny said. "I'll do the dishes and be on my way home."

"You aren't going home this early are you?" Steve asked.

"I really need to go on home," she said.

"I thought I might persuade you to take a walk in the garden with me. It's such a plesant evening and there's a cool breeze ," Steve said. "I will walk you home later."

"Why don't you do that Jenny? It is very nice outside and you've been busy all day," Mr. Newley said.

"Do, Jenny," Lora said. "The roses have such a sweet fragrance at this time of day. It will refresh you."

"I guess I could stay a short time," Jenny said.

Steve asked to be excused and got up from the table. He brought his dessert dish and his cup and set them on the counter. Then he turned to Jenny, bowed to her and extended his arm. "Shall we go, my lady?" he asked.

Jenny took his arm and they went walking to the rose garden. They hadn't walked very far when thay came to a bench. Steve said, "Why don't we sit for a while?"

Jenny sat down and Steve sat beside her.

"Jenny, I would like to talk to you. I've known you for several months now. I feel as if I know you very well and I feel you know me. As you know I am not married and have never been. I didn't think I would ever find the right woman for me. Well, now I know I was wrong. I have found her. Jenny, I love you and it would make me the happiest man in the world if you would be my wife," Steve said.

Jenny sat there stunned. Then tears began to flow down her cheeks. Steve took her in his arms and wiped the tears away. Then he kissed her.

"Steve," Jenny said, "I think I've loved you from the first day you arrived. I would be very happy to be your wife."

Steve reached into his pocket and took out a beautiful diamond ring. "When Newley and I took a trip the other day, I bought this for you. If you had not accepted my proposal, I would have sold it to Newley for Lora," he said.

He slipped the ring on Jenny's finger and kissed her again.

Jenny said, "I can't wait to show it to Mr. and Mrs. Newley."

She grabbed his hand and they went running into the house.

"What in the world is going on?" Lora asked.

Jenny showed her the ring and said, "Steve and I are getting married! Isn't the ring beautiful?"

Lora jumped up from the table and gave them both a hug. Mr. Newley rose from his chair and did the same.

"We're so happy for you!" They both said at the same time.

"Of course, you'll be married here," Lora said. "We'll decorate the house and have the reception after the wedding."

"It won't be for a while yet," Steve said. "Jenny and I will have to have a house and we have a lot things to decide. First we must tell her parents."

Jenny said, "Let's go and do that right now. I know they will be so happy for me. They really like Steve."

"I'll see you later," Steve said as they went out the door hand in hand.

"Take the truck," Mr. Newley called after them.

"We'll just walk," came back the reply.

They walked to Jenny's house hand in hand. They talked about the date of the wedding, where they would live and what kind of house they would build.

When they arrived at the Smithering house, Jerry, Jethro and Lettie were sitting on the front porch.

"What are you two so happy about?" Jerry asked.

Jenny showed them her ring and said, "Steve and I are getting married!"

Jerry and Jethro both shook Steve's hand and Lettie put her arms around Jenny and started to cry.

"I'm so happy for you, both Jenny," Lettie said. "I think Steve is a good man."

Jerry said, "I wondered when the two of you would wise up and see that you were perfect for each other."

Chapter 25

The Sheriff came over to "Pee Wee's" store one day and told him he needed to see Tom, Jim and Tim.

"If you'll wait just a few minutes they're coming by here. They had a few things to do, then they'll be here. Have a seat Sheriff, and tell us how things are going," "Pee Wee" said.

The Sheriff said, "Everything has been quiet for a change. My prisoners have been taken away to their new homes. The last I heard about the Russel boys they were really homesick and I don't think those two boys will ever give anybody any more trouble for the rest of their lives."

"Of course, Peters will never get out except in a pine box. It would take three life times for him to pay for all he's done."

Tom, Jim and Tim came walking in the door.

Tom said, "Look who's here. That mean Sheriff, who puts everybody in jail. Fellows, you better watch him.

Zeke, you'll behave now since he's here. Have you told the Sheriff about Slim making all of that whiskey?"

"Now, Tom, I ain't done no such a thing," Slim said.

The men really got a laugh out of that.

"Slim, sure thought he was a goner," "Pee Wee" said.

The Sheriff said, "You're safe, Slim. I don't have room for moonshiners."

"O.K., Slim, I guess you're safe for now," Jim said. "It was funny to see the look on your face, though."

"You two boys are just like your Daddy," Slim said. "You never know what's a coming out of your mouth."

"Sheriff, arrest that man for bad-mouthing," "Pee Wee" said.

"See I told you!" Slim said. The laughter started all over again.

The Sheriff said, "Tom, Tim and Jim, I need to talk to you. Let's go sit on the porch for a while."

The four men walked out of the store. When they were all seated the Sheriff started telling them the news. He pulled a sheet of paper from his pocket.

He said, "This is what we have been waiting for, boys. The lab report is back and now we know whose rifle fired the shots. Get the notebooks and let's see who it belongs to."

Tim went to his truck and got the three notebooks. They took the numbers that the lab had sent and compared them to the numbers in the notebooks.

They found a match almost immediately. The Sheriff said, "I don't believe this! There has to be a mistake. This person couldn't possibly be responsible. He has an air tight alibi."

Tom said, "We'll have to talk to him. There's no way around it."

Tim said, "Tom is right . There could be someone else there that did it. We have to go talk to them and get to the bottom of this. Something is sure not right. I don't know what it is but we have to dig until we come up with an answer from somebody"

The Sheriff said, "I had rather take a beating than have to make this trip, but we have no choice. It has to be done and we're the ones who have to do it. Jim, go tell "Pee Wee" we have some business we have to take care of. Don't tell him where we're going or why. Just tell him you'll see him later, but you don't know when."

Jim went into the store and told "Pee Wee" exactly what the Sheriff had told him to say. Then he turned and walked out.

The three men got in the Sheriff's car and went down the road.

The men at the store started guessing where they were going. None of them even knew what the four men had discussed on the front porch of the store.

"Jim sure had a serious look on his face," Zeke said.

"Where ever they're going, I'd say it's pretty serious stuff, from the looks of things," Slim said.

"Jim, was troubled," "Pee Wee" said. "I've seen that look to many times and he's always worried about something when he looks that way."

Chapter 26

The four men rode down the road until they came to the Newley house. They saw Jerry, Jethro, Mr. Newley and Steve at the barn, so they stopped. They pulled up to the gate and got out.

"Hello fellows, how are you today?" Mr. Newley asked.

"We're fine," the Sheriff said. "How are all of you? I see you've got Jerry back at work. How's your arm, Jerry?"

"It's almost good as new. The doctor says I'll have the full use of it in about three more weeks. It's still a little stiff and sore but it gets better every week," Jerry said.

"I need to talk to the three of you for a few minutes, if you've got the time," the Sheriff said.

Steve started to leave and Tim said, "There's no need for you to leave, Mr. Standford. We just need to make sure we've got our facts straight."

The Sheriff said, "Now, let me make sure this is what the three of you told us. You found the horse dead, Mr. Newley?"

"No, we had searched for the horse the night before, but didn't find it. Tom and Jim found it the next morning," Mr. Newley said.

"Jethro had come up that morning and we were going to look again. We hadn't left yet, when Jerry had come walking up here. When he started to open the gate to the barnyard we heard a shot and Jerry fell. It sounded like the shot had come from the hill across the road but we didn't see anybody. We got Jerry in my truck and carried him to the hospital."

"That's exactly what happened," Jethro said.

"Did any of you carry a weapon of any kind when you went looking for the horse the night before?" Tom asked.

"No", Jerry, Jethro and Mr. Newley all answered at the same time.

"We know that Steve wasn't here when any of this took place." the Sheriff said.

"No sir. I came about a week or so later," Steve said.

Mr. Newley said, "I need to tell you fellows something but I would really appreciate it if you kept it to yourselves. The Smithering family know about it but no one else does."

"Steve Standford is really Dr. Steve Sandford, a friend of mine since childhood. I went to see Steve and ask if he would come and stay here for a while. You see, my wife has been sick for almost a year now. Jenny, works for us you know. She started to notice several strange things that Lora was doing. She wouldn't leave her room for days, not even to eat. Then she would go outside and be gone for quite a while. She began to talk to her mother who has been dead for several years now. Her mother's family believe her husband killed her but before they could prove it, he died."

"I asked Steve to come and observe Lora and see if he could help her. He has treated her since he's been here and I'm glad to say that she has improved under his care. She is almost back to her old self and is now rational every day"

Steve spoke up, "Mrs. Newley had a nervous breakdown which is not uncommon, especially with women, who have been under a lot of stress for a while. The death of her mother and the circumstances of her death, after a while became to much for her to handle, so she snapped."

The Sheriff asked if Mrs. Newley had excess to the rifle.

"Yes, you remember when you came and asked to see my rifle? It wasn't in the cabinet where I always keep it. I found it in my wife's closet upstairs. That scared me because I was afraid she meant to hurt herself, so I went to get Steve," Mr. Newley said.

"We really need to talk to her. Is she well enough to do that?" Tim asked.

"She is still very fragile," Steve said. "The least thing could push her over the edge. Could you slip into the kitchen and I'll get her into the living room and see if she will talk to me about the rifle? Would that be alright?"

"That will be fine as long as we find out what we need to find out," Tim said.

"Let me and Steve get in the house and get Jenny and Lora in the living room, then just quietly come into the kitchen and listen," Mr. Newley said. "After you hear all you need to know, go back to the barn and Steve and I will come back out there. Wait in the hall of the barn."

The Secret of Jerry's Pride

Steve and Mr. Newley went to the house and Steve explained to Jenny what was going on.

Mr. Newley told Lora that they were in the living room and wanted her to join them.

"Yes dear," she said. "You know Steve and Jenny are getting married soon. Isn't it wonderful that they are getting married here in our home?"

"Yes, it is. They are made for each other, just as you and I were," Mr. Newley said.

"Sit on the couch with, Newley" Steve said. "Lora, I think it will help you if we talk about the past for a few minutes. Is that O.K. with you?"

"Yes, Steve, if you want me to do that," Lora said.

"Do you remember when you were feeling so bad?" Steve asked.

"Some of it I remember, some I don't," Lora said.

"Tell me what you remember, Lora," Steve said.

"I remember Randolph coming here and bringing the horse he rode. My husband left the house to look for him. I was afraid because I thought he had come to kill me like he killed Mama. I came downstairs and got the rifle to protect myself. I went out the back door and out across the garden and there he was with his horse. He started toward me and I shot him. The horse fell but Randolph got away."

"I knew he would come back. My husband went to the barn and I knew that Randolph would kill him. So I took the rifle and hid on the hill across the road. I saw him walking to the barn and when he opened the gate to go after my husband I shot him. He fell and two men took him away. I killed him, now he can't hurt us any more. He's gone, honey. He can't hurt us now. He took my mama and I wasn't going to let him take you, too. I couldn't live without you."

Then Lora started to cry and Mr. Newley took her in his arms and said, "It's fine, now, honey. I'm here and we're together. I won't leave you, ever. I'll always be with you. You will get well, now."

Jenny said, "Mrs. Newley, it's time for your medicine and you need to lie down and rest for a while. Mr. Newley, if you want to help her upstairs, I'll bring her medicine to her and she can take a nap before supper."

Mr. Newley picked Mrs. Newley up in his arms and carried her upstairs. When he got to their bedroom he sat her on the bed and went to her closet to get a gown for her. He helped her remove her dress and then put her gown on. Jenny came in with a glass of water and her mecicine. Mr. Newley gave it to her. Then gave her a kiss and he and Jenny went out of the room, softly closing the door behind them.

"I have to go to the barn, the Sheriff is waiting for me and I need to talk to Jerry," Mr. Newley said.

He walked to the barn where the men were waiting for him. He said, "Jerry, I am sorry. I had no idea. How can I ever make up to you for what happened?"

Jerry said, "Mr. Newley, you are not responsible. Mrs. Newley is sick, she is not responsible for what happened. She wasn't shooting at me, she was trying to protect you from what she saw as a killer. I will not bring any charges against her and I will not help anyone who does. Let it die. It's over."

The Sheriff said, "Mr. Newley, I'm so sorry. I've talked to the boys, Jerry, Jethro and Dr. Standford. We all agree that no crime has been commited and no charges can be brought where there is no crime. I hope Mrs. Newley gets better soon. She has a wonderful doctor and you have a great friend. If you need me I'll be here. I'm sorry again."

"This story stays here," Tim said.

Jim and Tom said, "There is no story to tell."

"Thank all of you so very much," Mr. Newley said. "You don't know how very much I appreciate this. You're a great bunch of men."

"We've got to get back to town and a group of agents will be going home tomorrow and I have a jail to run," the Sheriff said. "See you fellows later."

They got into the Sheriff's car and went back to town. From there the Sheriff went back to his town and Tim went with him.

Jim and Tom went home to spend some time with their parents.

All of the cases had been solved and closed.

Chapter 27

Life went on the way it had for several years. Jenny took care of Mrs. Newley every day. Some days were very good days, when it seemed to be the way she was when Jenny first came to work there. They would talk and laugh and work together in the rose garden.

Lora seemed to be very happy on those days. Sometimes these moods would last for a week, then without any warning her mood would turn into a totally different person. She would rant and rave for hours at a time over nothing.

Some days, she talked to her mother for hours as if her mother was there with her. At other times she talked to the man she had shot as if he was still alive. She never remembered that she had killed him, or at least thought she had.

Sometimes she acted as if she did not recognize anyone and was lost in an imaginary world of her own.

Dr. Standford was at a loss as what to try next. He had given her the strongest dose of medicine that he could give and at first it had helped her. Lately it seemed as if she was slipping farther and farther away from reality. He told Mr. Newley that if her condition continued to detoriate that he was afraid they would have to commit her to an instituion for her safety.

Mr. Newley said, "I will only do that as a last resort. I can't do that to Lora. There has to be something else we can do to help her. There has to be something!"

"There is something that I have heard about but I've never seen it tried, and I don't know if it would even work. Let me check into it and go see someone who knows more about it," Dr. Stanford said.

"I,ll go to New York to talk to this doctor that I know there. If anyone knows about this treatment, he will. He'll also know if it works or if there is something else we can try."

"I'll leave in the morning. I need to talk to Jenny before I leave."

Steve left the house after making sure Lora was asleep. He told Mr. Newley that he was going to see Jenny.

"Don't go to bed before I get back," Steve said. "If Lora gets up give her this sedative, that I'm leaving on the counter top in the kitchen. Don't let her out of your sight."

He got in his car and went to Jenny's house to talk to her.

He drove up to the front of her house, got out of his car and walked to the front door. He knocked on the door and Jenny came to the door and opened it.

She said, "Steve, what are you doing here? Is Lora sick?"

Steve said, "Nothing is wrong, Jenny. I just need to talk to you and your family. Is it O.K. for me to come in? Are your parents and Jerry still up?"

"Yes, come in," Jenny said. "Momma, Daddy and Jerry are in the kitchen. We were having some coffee and cake. Would you like some?"

"Yes, please," Steve said as he entered the kitchen. "Hello folks. I'm sorry to come this late, but I need to talk to all of you."

"I'm leaving for New York, in the morning," he said as he sat down.

"Why are you going to New York?" Jenny asked.

"I want to talk to a doctor I know who has a practice there," Steve said. "Lora is not getting any better and this doctor knows about a new procedure that is being tried. It has worked on one person, so far. I've never seen it done and I want to know more about it. We're going to have to try something else with Lora."

"I'm really worried about Lora. If there isn't a change soon I'm afraid she will only get to the point that she might harm herself or someone else," Steve said. "While I'm gone I want you to stay at the house, day and night. Newley won't be able to handle her alone. Jerry, I want you to stay at the house, too, just in case. Can you do that?" Steve asked. "I shoud be gone only for a week."

"Sure, Steve," Jenny said. "You know I'll do what I can to help. If she gets out of control what should I do?"

"I'll leave a very strong seditative that will knock her out for hours. Just be sure you only give her two tablets twice a day, two in the morning and two at night. Don't use them unless she gets to the point she won't listen to you."

"Doc, I'll stay up at the house, but I'll be busy working with the horses during the day. I'll be there at night," Jerry said.

Jenny's mother said, "I'll go up there every morning and stay with Jenny during the day while Jerry is working. I won't leave until Jerry is through with his work. With all of us helping we'll make it fine."

"Thank all of you so much," Steve said. "I need to get back. I told Newley I wouldn't be gone very long. He might need me. Will you walk me to the car, Jenny? Goodnight, folks. See all of you in a week."

Jenny walked Steve to his car. "I'm going to miss you, Jenny," Steve said as he took her in his arms and kissed her. "You know I love you."

"I love you, too, Steve. Just hurry back home," Jenny said.

Steve got in his car and drove back to the Newley house. When he got there he got out and went into the house.

Mr. Newley was sitting in the living room waiting for Steve.

"Lora is still asleep. She hasn't been awake since you've been gone," Mr. Newley said.

"That's good," Steve said. "I need to talk to you. While I'm gone, Jenny and Jerry are going to stay here with you. They'll be here day and night. Jenny's mother is coming up every morning and stay until Jerry finishes working and then she'll go home. If Lora gets worse you'll need their help. I've told Jenny what to do if that happens, listen to her and do as she says."

"I'll do whatever you say, Steve," Mr. Newley said. "Just find out something that will help my Lora. I may not see you before you leave in the morning. I'll stay with Lora until Jenny gets here. I think I'll go to bed now. I'll see you when you get back. Goodnight."

"Goodnight, Newley," Steve said. "Be careful while I am gone. I'll be back in a week, hopefully with help for Lora."

Chapter 28

The next morning before daylight Steve left for New York. He knew that it would take at least two days of hard driving to reach his friends hospital. He would have to stop to catch a few hours of rest before he got there.

About noon, on the third day, he pulled up in front of the hospital. He got out of his car and went inside. He stopped at the front desk and asked if Dr. Carl Strom was in. The nurse at the desk said that he was.

"Would you please ring his office and tell him that Dr. Steve Standford would like to speak with him?" Steve asked.

The nurse did as she was asked, and soon a very tall, strong man came walking down the hall.

"Steve, old boy! What are you doing here?" the man asked as he gave Steve a bear hug.

"I came to see if you were still playing doctor," Steve said. "Carl, it is good to see you, again. You haven't changed a bit."

"You haven't changed much either," Carl said. "Maybe got a little better looking, if that's possible. Now tell me why you are really here and what can I do to help you."

Steve said, "You know me to well, my friend. I do need your help. I have a very sad case and I've done all I know to do, and it doesn't seem to help."

"Let's go get some lunch and talk it over. I have the afternoon off today, so after lunch we can go to my house. You look like you could use some rest," Carl said.

They ate lunch at a small diner about a block from Carl's house. After lunch they went on to Carl's house and went inside.

Steve told Carl all about everything that had happened and about Lora. He also asked about the treatment he had heard about.

Carl said, "There is a new treatment that I've seen tried twice. In both cases it worked, but I don't think it would work for everyone. It's called hypnosis. You put a person in a deep sleep and talk to them about things they have blocked from their mind. If you can get them to remove that block and talk about what happened, sometimes after they have faced what has happened, they get O.K."

"Like I said, I've only seen a couple of cases done, and they both worked, but the next person they try it on might not work at all."

Carl continued, "It's a form of hypnosis but it must be done by a specialist, who has studied the technique of this particular procedure. It's only been tried on people as a last resort. We don't know what might happen if something went wrong. It's still in the expermintal stage. Steve, are you sure you've tried everything else?"

"Carl, this patient is also my best friend's wife. I've done everything I know, except shock treatments. I don't want to subject her or her husband through that, if I have a choice," Steve said.

"Is there any way she could come here?" Carl asked.

"I really am afraid that would drive her even farther away. Really, I don't think she could stand the trip," Steve said. "Could you possibly go to her? Money is no object, in this case. Maybe if you saw her and observed her in her own environment, you could think of some treatment I haven't thought of yet."

"I do have some time coming to me, that I can take anytime," Carl said. "All of my patients are at a point that any of our doctors could take over their cases. Do you think three weeks or a month would be enough time?"

"That would be wonderful," Steve said.

"Let me talk to Dr. Walters and see if that can be arranged," Carl said. I"ll let you know tonight. By the way where are you staying?"

"At the hotel about a block from here, I'm in Room 212," Steve said. "I need to get going. I'm going to have something to eat in the hotel dinning room and then go to my room to rest. It was a long trip and I haven't really stopped since I got here. It's a long trip back and I need to get started back in the morning. See you later, and Carl, thank you. This means a lot to me."

"Talk to you later, Steve," Carl said. "You'd do the same for me."

Steve left Carl's house and drove to the hotel.

After eating a sandwich and having a cup of coffee he went to his room to rest until Carl called later.

Around six o'clock someone knocked on Steve's door. He went to answer it immediately. Carl was standing there.

"Come in," Steve said. "I wasn't expecting to see you this soon. I thought you might call."

"I finished earlier than uaual. I had to drive by here on my way home, so I decided to just stop. I thought we could get a bite to eat in the dinning room downstairs and I wouldn't have to fix dinner when I got home," Carl said.

"That sounds fine," Steve said. "I only had a sandwich for lunch."

They took a table in the hotel dinning room and ordered their dinner.

Their dinner was brought to their table and they began to talk as they ate.

Carl said, "I talked to Dr. Walters this afternoon and got permission to take some time off. He also told me about a medicine that we could try. He said that sometimes it would work when nothing else would. I'm taking a good supply with me so we can try it. Maybe it will do the trick. I sure hope so. What time are you leaving in the morning?"

"I thought I'd leave around 5:00 o'clock, if that is O.K. with you," Steve said.

By this time they had finished their dinner. They got up from the table and paid their bill and walked out into the lobby.

"I'll be by your house to pick you up around five fifteen in the morning," Steve said.

"I'll be ready," Carl said. "Get a good nights rest and I'll see you in the morning, Goodnight."

"Goodnight," Steve said, as he entered the elevator on his way to his room.

Chapter 29

After getting a good night's rest Steve got up the next morning, took a shower, got dressed and after paying his hotel bill, went to pick up Carl.

When he pulled into the driveway at Carl's house, Carl came out the door with a suitcase. He checked the door to be sure that it was locked, then came to the car. Steve got out, opened the trunk of the car and put Carl's suitcase in along beside his own. He shut the lid of the trunk and got back in the car. Carl opened the passenger's door and got in and closed the door.

"Are you ready for a long ride?" Steve asked. "I thought we'd stop for breakfast after we got on our way."

"That sounds good to me," Carl said. "I didn't take time for breakfast. I wanted to make sure I brought the medicine that Dr. Walters gave me for your patient. I sure hope it works for her, as it has for others."

"You'll really like Newley," Steve said, "You'd like Lora too, if she was herself. They're two of the nicest people you'd ever hope to meet. There is also a very special lady I'm anxious for you to meet. Her name is Jenny, and she is looking after Lora for me, while I'm gone. She's going to become Mrs. Steve Standford, as soon as Lora gets better."

"Well, you really shocked me with that one. I had no idea you would ever give up your freedom," Carl said. "Jenny must really be something, to snag you."

"She's one special lady. She has beauty and brains and the sweetest nature you'll ever see," Steve said.

"I'm happy for you, Steve," Carl said. "I just wish I could be so lucky. So far the women I've met are either after your money or they're already married."

"When you least expect it, you'll meet the one for you," Steve said. "I had given up and stopped looking, when I met Jenny."

They had driven about fifty miles when they pulled into a little diner for breakfast.

After finishing their breakfast and several cups of coffee, they were on their way again.

Two days later they pulled up to the Newley house. It was about eight o'clock in the morning. Jenny came out on the porch to meet Steve. After he had given Jenny a kiss, he turned to Carl and said, "Jenny, I would like for you to meet a friend of mine, Carl Strom. Carl, this is Jenny Smithering."

"It's nice to meet you Mr. Strom," Jenny said extending her hand.

"It's nice to meet you, too, Jenny," Carl said. "By the way I am a doctor, like Steve, and please call me Carl."

Steve went back to the car and got the suitcases out of the trunk. He brought them to the porch and Carl took his.

Jenny held the door for them to enter the house. They sat the suitcases down in the foyer.

"Everybody is having breakfast in the dinning room," Jenny said. "I'll set a couple more plates and pour you some coffee. I made plenty to eat because I thought you might get home about this time."

Jenny got the plates and poured the coffee while Steve introduced Carl to everybody. Then they all sat down to eat. Lora was down for breakfast today. She seemed to be in pretty good condition.

"Carl, have you known Steve very long?" Lora asked.

"Yes, we were in college together," Carl said.

"Oh, are you a friend of my husband, too?" Lora asked.

"I know your husband, but I wasn't friends with him like I was with Steve because he and I didn't have the same classes," Carl said.

"Honey, do you remember Carl?" Lora asked.

"Yes, I remember seeing him in college, but as he said we didn't have any classes together." Mr. Newley said.

Steve, asked, "Lora, how have you been feeling since I've been gone?"

"Steve, I didn't know you were gone until day before yesterday. I had been sleeping a lot," Lora said.

Jenny spoke up, "Miss Lora was very tired for a few days. We had been working pretty hard in the rose garden. She probably did more work than she should have."

"Speaking of the rose garden, honey, would you walk out with me to see the roses?" Lora asked.

"Yes, dear, if you promise just to look at the roses and sit on the garden bench with me for a while," Mr. Newley said.

"I promise, if you promise to recite for me the poem you did last night." Lora said smilling.

"You drive a hard bargain, my love, but I promise," Mr. Newley said as he helped her up from the table.

Lora said, "Please excuse us, but my sweetheart and I are going to the rose garden to steal a few kisses."

Afer they had left the room Jenny poured some coffee and sat back down. "It's wonderful to see her like that again. This is two days in a row now," she said.

"How have the other days been?" Steve asked.

Jenny said, "She had a couple of really rough days. She would not let Mr. Newley out of her sight. She was so afraid. Mama and I did every thing we could to calm her but Mr. Newley was the only one she would let near her."

Steve said, "Jenny, Carl is a doctor and he has a new medicine we want to try with Lora, because we think it will help her. Carl is going to be staying here for a while with us."

"Oh, if only it will help her. It breaks my heart to see her go through such torment," Jenny said.

Carl said, "Today she seems to be perfectly fine. You wouldn't know she had a problem at all."

About that time Lora and Mr. Newley came back into the kitchen.

Lora said, "Jenny our work paid off. The roses have never been more beautiful."

Mr. Newley said, "They are almost as beautiful as my wife. Notice I said "almost" as beautiful."

"Jenny, I hope Steve is as loving with you as my husband is to me," Lora said.

Jenny's face blushed a deep red and Steve laughed. "If I'm not, she has an awfully big rolling pen and she knows how to use it," he said.

"Carl, are you a married man?" Mr. Newley asked.

"No, I'm afraid I haven't been as lucky as you and Steve," Carl said. "I haven't been able to find a woman as beautiful as these two ladies. If I do find one, believe me, I won't give up until she's mine."

"Thank you," Lora said. "By the way, welcome to our home. We're glad you're here and hope you stay for a while."

"With your permission, I would be happy to spend some time here. It's a beautiful place and so very peaceful. It's like being in heaven, after being in so much noise in New York," Carl said.

Steve said, "Newley, I would like to talk to you and Lora for a few minutes, if I may."

Mr. Newley said, "Let's go into the living room. That way Jenny can get her work done without us being in her way."

Carl said, "Jenny, if you don't mind, I'd like another cup of coffee. I'll stay here out of your way."

Jenny said, "you won't be in my way, Carl. I'll get your coffee."

She poured him a cup of coffee and started cleaning the table.

Soon she had the dishes all washed, dried and put away. Then she refilled her cup with coffee and sat down at the table with Carl.

Meanwhile, in the living room Steve was telling Lora and Mr. Newley about the new medication he wanted to start giving her.

"I wanted to know how you both feel about this before we started it. What do you think Lora?" Steve asked.

"Sure, Steve, if you think it will help me, I'll be happy to try it." Lora said.

"Steve, Lora and I both trust you with our lives. If you think this will help her, start her on it immediately. She hasn't had her medicine this morning." Newley said.

"You will only take one pill in the morning, one at noon and one at bed time. You won't have to worry about when to take it, because I will give it to you at the right time. It's 10 o'clock now, so it's to close to lunch for the morning dose. We'll take your first dose at noon," Steve said. "I think after a week you will be feeling like your old self again."

Later Steve told Carl what he had told the Newley's. Carl agreed that he had chosen the right doseage for Lora. They would both observe Lora and then compare their findings.

Chapter 30

By noon Lora was very nervous and restless. Her mind wasn't as clear as it had been earlier in the day.

When they sat down for lunch Steve gave Lora her pill and a glass of water. He told her to drink the full glass of water after she had taken the pill. Then she ate lunch.

Steve and Carl both watched Lora during lunch. At the beginning of lunch her hands were trembling and she seemed somewhat confused.

By the time lunch was over and they were all having dessert and coffee, her hands were steady and the confusion was gone. They were both sure they were on the right track.

That afternoon they all sat in the living room talking. Steve told some jokes and none of them enjoyed them more than Lora. She had laughed more that afternoon than she had in a long time.

Later in the afternoon she and Newley went for a short walk. She did not take a nap and seemed to have more energy.

Jenny prepared dinner and they all sat down to eat. She had golden brown pork chops, green beans, mashed potatoes, sliced tomatoes and cole slaw, along with home made rolls. For dessert she had made a peach cobbler served with a scoop of homemade vanilla ice cream.

"Do you have a sister?" Carl asked Jenny.

"No, but I have a good friend I'd like you to meet," Jenny said. "She is a school teacher and pretty as a picture. I'll invite her for dinner one night next week."

Lora thought that was a great idea. She thought they would make the ideal couple.

Steve carried Jenny home and they discussed Lora on the way.

Steve asked, "Jenny, could you see any difference in Lora this afternoon?"

"I haven't seen her the way she has been today, in a long time. She was the Lora I knew before everything happened. I believe this medication is really going to work," Jenny said.

"If she continues to improve for the next month, we should be able to begin to make plans for our future," Steve said. "We'll start making plans about the type of house we want and where we want it to be. Start thinking about your dream house because that is what I want to build for you."

"As long as we're together I can live in any house," Jenny said.

By that time they had reached Jenny's parents house. Steve walked Jenny to the door. They kissed goodnight and Steve went on his way to the Newleys.

After he returned to the Newley house, he went inside and went to get Lora's medication.

Soon he returned with a glass of water and her medication. He said, " Lora, here is your pill for tonight. Go on and take the pill and drink all of the glass of water."

Lora did as Steve told her and handed him the empty glass. Shortly after she and her husband went to bed.

Carl said, "Well Steve, this medication seems to be doing the trick. I had an idea this afternoon that I would like to try, with your permission."

"What do you have in mind?" Steve asked.

"I would like to try talking to Lora about her childhood, and see what kind of reaction I get," Carl said.

"You have my permission to try anything that you feel will help Lora's case. Her childhood is a part of her problem, it's true, but do you think she has been on the medication long enough to start with therapy?" Steve asked.

"I don't think it will harm her in any way. Sooner or later she is going to have to come to terms with what happened during her childhood. The sooner she learns to do that, the sooner she will start to heal," Carl said.

"Let me think about it overnight and I'll give you an answer in the morning." Steve said. "Are you ready to turn in? I don't know about you, but I am tired."

"Yep, it's been a very long day and I'm tired too. Let's hit the hay." Carl said.

The night was very quiet and passed uneventful.

Chapter 31

The next morning Jenny got to the Newley house around seven thirty. Steve and Carl were up and having a cup of coffee in the kitchen when she walked in. She walked over and gave Steve a kiss.

"Good morning, gentlemen," Jenny said.

"Good morning," they said at the same time.

"Why don't you sit and have a cup of coffee with us before you start breakfast?" Steve asked.

"That sounds like a great idea," Jenny said as she poured herself a cup of coffee and refilled Carl's and Steve's cups.

At about eight thirty Lora and Mr. Newley came downstairs.

"Good morning," Lora said.

"Good morning," the three at the table said.

"Jenny, would you please pour Lora and me a cup of coffee?" Mr. Newley asked.

"How are you feeling this morning Lora?" Steve asked.

"I feel better than I have felt in a long time in the morning," Lora said. "I'm hungry as a wolf, Jenny. I'd like some scrambled eggs, some country ham, hot biscuits and grits, please."

"You haven't asked for a breakfast like that in a long time," Jenny said. "I'll be happy to prepare your breakfast. How does that sound to you all?"

"Great!" all three men said at the same time.

Steve left the table, but was back in a few minutes with Lora's medicine. He ran her a glass of water from the kitchen faucet and handed her the pill and the glass of water. She took the medicine and drank the glass of water.

"Thank you, Steve," she said. "Now, I can have my coffee, and a good breakfast. Then a stroll in the garden with my love. Who could ask for more?"

They all sat down to a wonderful breakfast.

After breakfast Lora and her husband went for a walk in the rose garden, while Jenny cleared the table and did the dishes. Steve and Carl kept her company while they drank coffee.

Later after Lora aand Newley came inside, they all went into the living room.

They had only been there for a few minutes when Carl said, "Lora, tell me about your childhood."

Lora started talking, "My Mother was a very beautiful woman. My father died when we were very young. Later my Mother remarried a man I didn't care for. He was a greedy man and married my Mother for her money."

"Later she died and I think he killed her, but I could never prove it. For many years it almost drove me into a nervous break down."

"I met my husband and we were married and moved away. I don't know what finally happened to my stepfather except I heard that he had died. Since his death I have not worried about him any more. I am completely happy for the first time since my father's death."

"Do you ever feel angry at him or think you see him?" Carl asked.

"I used to, a long time ago but I no longer do. He is dead, so that ended all of my feelings about him, one way or the other. I no longer think about him," Lora said.

"Do you remember being sick for several months lately?" Steve asked.

"I haven't felt well, but I haven't been sick. I had a fever or something and I don't remember that time but I am fine now," Lora said.

"And you no longer feel anger toward your stepfather?" Carl asked.

"I don't feel anything toward him. He is out of my life forever," Lora said.

"Do you remember Jerry being shot at not long ago?" Steve asked.

"No! Was he hurt?" Lora asked. "That must have happened while I was sick. Do they know who did it and why?"

"It was a freak accident possibely a hunters stray bullet. Jerry is fine," Mr. Newley said.

"That's wonderful, that's he's fine," Lora said.

"Steve, when are you and Jenny getting married?" Lora asked.

"I have to move my practice here. Get us a place and build our house," Steve said.

"We'll give you a place to build your house, if you want it," Mr. Newley said.

"I would love that," Jenny said. "That way I would still be near Lora."

"If that's what you want, then that's the way it will be," Steve said.

Carl and Steve discussed the session they had with Lora and agreed the medicine was working. They would keep her on it and they didn't think it would ever return.

Chapter 32

The dream house of Jenny and Steve was built just down the road from the Newley home. Steve had moved his practice to Newleyville and he also had a partner. Carl had met the pretty school teacher and they were planning a wedding later in the year.

Steve and Jenny were married in the Newley house. Newley was the best man and Lora was Jenny's Matron of Honor.

They have a beautiful home built some what in the same style as the Newley house.

Jerry still trains horses for Mr. Newley and last year they had the Grand Champion. Jerry is working with a new horse he thinks will become a Grand Champion in a year or two.

Jerry is still a bachlor but he has been seeing a girl in town for the last year.

The men still gather at "Pee Wee's" store as they always have.

Lora is in very good health, both mentally and physical and she still takes her mecicine faithfully each day. She and Mr. Newley are a very happy couple.

Every once in a while the Sheriff drops by for a visit with the Newley's. They have become the best of friends and Lora still has no idea of the secret the Sheriff and her husband share.

Jerry often visits the monument in the back pasture and thinks of what he and Jerry's Pride could have become but maybe it wasn't meant to be, that way.

The Secret of Jerry's Pride lies buried under the monument and in the hearts of a handful of people, where it will remain forever hidden.

The End

www.ingramcontent.com/pod-product-compliance
Lightning Source LLC
LaVergne TN
LVHW011944070526
838202LV00054B/4788